EDEN

EDEN

SONIA OVERALL

WEATHERGLASS BOOKS

To James, with love and thanks

It begins with few expectations. At least that's what you believe. He pushes open the door and the sap takes hold and rises in his chest. He sharpens his pencils, sets to work. Your face blossoms. Your shoulders straighten, your fingers tingle. You have hope. You have definition. It shows. He sees it, pursues it.

You are another face. It is, of course, a wonderful face. He decides to like it, and to despise it a little. He decides to play a little game.

He is gun-shy. He is weary with hope. He has written so many wonderful faces and many that were not so wonderful, and he is not sure yet what will become of yours. But in that moment, you spark into life. So he begins.

1.

Max O'Grady: third year, BA English and American Lit. He was in her lectures last year, one with questions, with a hand always first in the air. Good. This is the kind of student Pen likes. She noticed him then. Erratum: she registered him then. But she's truly noticed him now.

She has noticed other students before. Boys. Boys enter the seminar room. Soft edges morphing; the faces of hatchling men. Just kids really. Noticing them meant nothing.

It's late. Two hours of a guest speaker from Essex. Andy Something. She has already forgotten. 'Magic Realism and its Heritage'. Not her heritage. Not her thing. Her turn to represent the department though.

Pen does not represent the department often; she is usually pairing socks and speed-washing Toby's sports kit. It is a rare evening on campus. She is famished. In the week she eats early with Toby; now her blood sings with over-salted peanuts scooped in handfuls, with tepid college Shiraz. Warmth of the hand around a thin plastic beaker, sweat gathering in palm creases, itching for escape. (Do Not Squeeze.) She wills it over: home, home, home speed. Nate may have saved her some supper. If not there is always soup. Always.

Andy Something stutters to a climax. Steve Saunders, presiding, hands waving (jazz hands, Jacobean jewelled hands, stagehands) calls for questions. Hands go into the air. One hand is that of Max O'Grady. He asks Andy Something if magic realism isn't just giving the author a free pass to write their way out of anything. Andy Something laughs. Max O'Grady persists. Andy Something evokes the power of the absurd, the boundaries between worlds blurring. Then why not just call it fantasy? Max O'Grady says. The students either side of Max roll their eyes. Andy Something takes another question.

Then the questions stop and the hands clap and the wine comes out again. The students bunch grape-like into groups. Some of them court Andy Something with words and wide looks and grave, gratifying nods. They are mostly postgrads. Pen looks around for the black-haired third year with the narrowed eyes, the awkward questions, the advancing aggressive tone. Mary Dene from Comparative Literature, faculty lanyard fully emblazoned, nags her about a new study group; Pen's input would be valuable. Pen nods. Pen thinks: Max O'Grady. A rose is a rose is a rose by any other name. She marked his first-year essay on Joyce; gave it a first. That was unusual. She'd remarked it at the time. A first grade in a first assignment in the first year of study. Rare. Rare and flowering. Then those *Lit in Context* lectures last year. How are his grades now? She looks around again. Did he leave? Steve Saunders, hands describing cartwheels, mutters about increasing student expectations. Pen considers Steve Saunders' own expectations. Professor? Head of School? She squeezes the plastic beaker until it cracks and thanks Andy Something for an interesting evening.

It is raining hard. She stops at the office to collect files. First-year essays, second marking. Marking: there is always marking. Interminable drudge. Charlady of academia. The marking obscures all; a vertiginous creeper engulfing her book on

Gertrude Stein, *All this and not ordinary*. But the ordinary takes over, the ordinary wins. Research is like the summer: a distant memory, a lost love.

Files, email, shut down, lights off, door locked. Pen runs across the floodlit car park, dodging puddles, noticing and noticing and noticing Max O'Grady.

Max stands in the corner of the car park in the rain.

Pen knows it is him. She knows it from his height, from his black hair, collar-length, flattening in the deluge. She knows it from the red satchel, balanced on a bouncing knee as he grilled Andy Something, now a sling of colour over his shoulder. She gets into the car, shakes off her hood, puts the bag of files on the back seat. She has escaped, leaving Steve Saunders to carry the baton. No after-talk dinner. The rain smashes on the bonnet. No talking to Andy Something about Rushdie, no listening to Steve's stories about Samuel Beckett. No wanting to drink all the wine and holding off because of the car. No polite endurance. No sharing of lifts or deliverance of Andy Something into the questionable embrace of the County Hotel's purple plush reception at the end of the evening, driving through the incessant bloody rain at eleven, dry-mouthed and yawning, Nate waiting, grumbling. Escape.

Pen starts the car. The wipers beat wearily. Under the floodlights Max does not move. He stands, hands in pockets, looking out across the wide wet field.

She thinks: What *is* he doing? She thinks: He will catch a chill. She thinks: He was angry. Those were angry questions. Why?

Then she thinks: I wonder if he's all right.

Her feet are wet; she needs new boots. She wants to go home, to be at home already, to be transported there without having to find a place to park the car halfway up the road and get soaked walking back to the house.

She should leave. She should leave him there in the rain. She drives over and lowers the window.

Max? she says. It is Max, isn't it?

She knows who it is. Betray nothing, her voice says. Reveal nothing. A boy in the rain, a boy drenched and listless and lovely in the rain. His eyes are no longer narrow. His pinched nose is a funnel, a slipstream, a sloping eddy. He is soaked. His hair curls a wet cowlick on his cheek: a flapper swirl, a Regency flourish. Rain streams from wet hair into open collar. She thinks: Oh.

Are you all right? she says. You're getting very wet.

He shrugs. It's just rain, he says.

It's freezing, she says. Do you need a lift? I can take you into town.

He looks at the puddles. Behind him rain bounces hard on college steps.

Okay, he says. Okay, thanks.

She drives. The rain beats. Max O'Grady is silent as they reach the railway crossing. The lights start to flash; Pen stops the car. As the gates descend Max O'Grady puts his head in his hands and sobs.

Pen doesn't think. Her hand is on the boy's shoulder. He takes hold of it and squeezes: squeezes, presses, takes it between his own, moulding, kneading. Sorry, he says, sorry, sorry. I'm so sorry.

Don't be, she says.

Then his hands are at his eyes and her own lies idle in his lap.

A dropped glove. She places it swiftly on the steering wheel.

He sighs, bellows emptying. He shakes his head, his shoulders, stirring himself. She thinks: He is sloughing off the moment. He is wiping me away. She thinks: But I am still here. I am waiting.

I'm sorry, he says. My girlfriend dumped me. My dad phoned to tell me the dog died. I got a fifty-six for my last essay. A fifty-six! I made a tit out of myself at the talk. I'm going to quit the course.

In the heat of the car his wet clothes steam softly. He is a freshly washed dog: soap powder, damp leather jacket. Pen fishes a tissue from her pocket. He takes it.

I don't even know why I'm doing this course, he says. My English A-level teacher told me I should do it. I'm only here because I didn't know what else to do. I got good marks the last two years but I feel like such a fraud. I mean, why am I doing this?

Rain rattles on the roof. The wipers squeak and slosh, squeak and slosh. The train clicks past slowly. Pen takes a deep breath.

Do not go, she wants to say. She thinks: Do not go because now the world is better with you in it and you are too fine. She thinks: You need this. I need this. She thinks: Now we are in this together.

She does not say these things.

What's your favourite text so far? she asks. I mean, that you've discovered since you got here?

I don't know, he says. He blows his nose; muted, respectful. Is there a right answer?

Your answer is the right answer, she says.

I liked Joyce's *Dubliners*.

Good, she says, but don't tell me that just because I love it and I teach it and you probably read my critiques of it for your first-year essay.

Okay, he says. Rumbled.

He twitches a smile. The train gates judder and lift: his face in pulsing light of signal crossing, street lamps, passing cars, play of colours. Her hand on the steering wheel opens, grips, opens. She thinks: A beautiful boy, a beautiful boy smiling. She thinks: No more, no no no more. She drives on.

What else have you read lately? she says, to the rail tracks, to the flicking white road strip. Did anything strike you?

Slaughterhouse-Five. Um, Raymond Carver's short stories. *Midnight's Children.*

Ha! And you gave Andy from Essex a hard time?

I know, he says. I feel bad now. But he did piss me off.

She thinks: Exoticism, symbolism, colonialism. Ismismism. She thinks: Spinning dials, unclocked overtime. She thinks: He rather pissed me off too.

Look, she says, don't worry about the talk. Speakers expect to be goaded. Whenever you give a talk there's always someone that does it. He won't be offended.

Max O'Grady laughs. A bus slows at the traffic lights and she brakes behind it to glance at him: open mouth over straight teeth, stretched neck, tender lump of Adam's apple. The lights allow her to linger longer, *go red go red, laugh white.*

That's me, he says. He turns in the seat to look straight at her, eyes on full blaze. Did I do that to you? he says. In your lectures?

Do what, she says, ask annoying questions?

Yes.

No, she says. You usually asked sensible questions. Although sometimes you asked them a little – forcibly.

Right, he says.

He faces forward again. The bus pulls out. Pen follows.

Actually, she says, I was pleased to have you there. At least I knew someone was listening.

Max O'Grady asks to be dropped off on the east side of town. He points out a pub and they pull up outside. The rain eases a little. They sit in the car. The wipers continue to squeak and slosh, squeak and slosh. They continue to sit.

Thank you, he says.

You're welcome, she says.

She thinks: This is the moment something happens. This is the point of exchange. He opens the door a little, hesitates. The light comes on above his head. His wet hair so black it is blue. His eyes so blue they are almost black. She thinks: Beautiful boy, blue boy, goodbye.

Sorry I was such an idiot, he says.

You're anything but, she says.

Thanks.

He swings a leg out of the door.

You can come and talk to me, she says. Whenever you need to. You know where my office is.

Thanks.

Don't quit, Max, she says. Just get drunk and sleep it off. You'll be fine.

He gets out, unfurling onto the kerb, black legs and red satchel and jacketed elbows. He turns to close the door and his face hangs there and she thinks, oh fleeting thought, of taking this elfish face in her hands, of kissing this tapering chin.

Look, he says, would it be okay to come and see you tomorrow? I mean, should I book a tutorial?

Just come to my office, she says. My timetable is on the door.

Thanks, he says.

Then he is gone.

Driving home she reaches out, touches the passenger seat. The fabric is sodden. A damp tissue balled up on the dashboard. She thinks: *In loco parentis.* This boy needs someone to look out for him.

She thinks: It was only the rain. The rain is wrong, *wet weather means an open window.*

She thinks: Too much Stein. Too easily led, too ready to make connections where there are none. But there is a connection. There was. She is sure of that.

She thinks: He needed and she was there and that is all.

The next morning the cat is sick on the stairs. Nate leaves early for a meeting, buttered toast in hand, glancing kiss goodbye. Toby dawdles over breakfast, delays brushing his teeth, loses a shoe. Pen drops him at the gates and sits for an hour in traffic.

She sees it from across the hall: a note pinned to her office door. Folded square of blue-lined notebook paper, spiral-edged. Student paper.

Dear Penelope
Called by on the way to my lecture to say thanks. Sorry I missed you. I won't quit. I think I chose the wrong classes. I'm seeing my tutor today about switching to your Modernism module.
I really did like Dubliners, you know.
Max O.

Imagine, she thinks. Imagine not imagining. Do not imagine. Stop it, right now.

That afternoon she sees Steve Saunders in the corridor. He is wearing his uniform white-shirt-black-jacket. The shirt collar nonchalantly frayed. The black jacket no longer very black. He holds up a hand for her to stop.

A third-year student has been asking me if he can swap classes, he says, frowning, brown brows bowing. He wants to join your Modernism seminar.

Ah, she begins, I wondered—

I told him it's out of the question. It's far too late into term.

Perhaps—

You know how I feel about this, Penelope. We shouldn't encourage students to move. Third-year choices are so important and I don't want any of the others jumping ship.

Pen nods. Pen shakes her head. Pen enquires about dinner with Andy Something. She looks at the black buttons on Steve Saunders' jacket. One of them has been sewn back on with blue thread, oh, tender button. There is something hopeless about Steve Saunders which she once found endearing. The cultivated shabbiness. The shadows beneath his spectacles. *Imagine eyeglasses*; yes, she has. Imagined them in isolation on bedside tables, imagined their arms folded into bookmarks. Imagined Steve Saunders is not so hopeless, not so fragile, the crumpled librarian look more Larkin than Prufrock.

Was it Max O'Grady? she says. I'm rather concerned about him.

Steve Saunders rubs his chin. Hand grates against stubble. Max is getting lazy, he says, or distracted. His essay on Hemingway was dreadful.

Pen looks hard at the lint dusted around Steve Saunders' jacket pocket. Maybe Max has lost interest in his current class, she says.

Maybe he doesn't like the way I mark, he says. Either way, moving classes will only disrupt him further.

~

Pen thinks this is the end of Max O'Grady. The week passes and the weekend passes and then it is Tuesday. The rain and the damage and the face that lingered linger less brightly. She gathers the papers for another seminar: third year, Modernism module. She will give them Gertrude Stein. Today her work is her love, is raising its colours, flourishes. She gathers notes and handouts, her *Gertrude Stein: A Reader* littered with yellow Post-it flags, bristling with attention. Jacket, bag, books, door. At the door, fist raised to knock, the boy: Max O'Grady.

Hello, he says.

Hello and hello and hello. She is about to leave and he knows it and that is why he has come. Steve Saunders has told him that it is too late to change courses but could she, may he, would she, record some of the sessions anyway? He holds out a little metallic tube; his friend Jay Fisher is in her group and he will do it, press the buttons, oh tender, record them, the discussions, if she doesn't mind. She nods and listens and takes him in again and the blueness and blackness of him and says, yes, she could do that, she could check with the group and she could do it, start the recording, pass the recorder on to Jay Fisher at the end of today's session. She could do that. She could.

Max O'Grady beams and leans in the doorway, hand on red satchel strap, thankful, polite, mouth succulent, lupine. Oh, she thinks. Oh oh no. Then he is gone again and she closes the door behind her and locks it and checks her watch, five minutes, breathes, leaves. So. So.

Max's recorder in her jacket pocket. Through the corridors and down the steps she feels it swing hard against her hip as she walks. *Thup. Thup. Thup.*

1943: Cuba

It was Christmas and he was alone. That had never happened before.

The boys were with their mothers. Marty was away playing journalist. Europe was at war, she kept telling him. The world was at war. When was he going to do something about it? Well, he had done something. He had fixed up *Pilar* and rigged her out with equipment for submarine patrols and stocked the boat with guns and hand grenades. He and his crew had spent weeks trolling around the Gulf Stream looking for tin fish, watching for drop points where Fascist sympathizers might leave supplies. Marty knew what he'd been doing. She laughed at his equipment and his grenades. She said he spent more time on the boat drinking and playing poker than carrying out intelligence operations. What the hell did she know about it? He was always on the lookout. And he'd spent plenty of offshore evenings sitting up late with an oil lamp correcting the manuscript of her novel. She didn't mind him doing that.

He was lonely. He wasn't ashamed to admit it.

At least his wife wrote to him when she was away. And her letters were kinder than she was. They'd spent a good deal of time apart writing each other letters. Their courtship letters were full of longing. Longing only came when they were apart.

When they were first together he had written to her about her skin and her hair and how their intimate friend, Mr Scrooby, couldn't wait to wink at her again. That seemed like a long time ago. He wanted her all the time he couldn't have her and for a good while when they were first married. She was tall and taffy-haired with slim legs and striking features. She was afraid of nothing and she cared about everyone else and wanted to change the plight of the poor and make palaces out of slums. Shortly after they married they went through China together while the South Sea war was breaking around them and she was sickened by the filth and the way the poor lived. He said, what if the poor like it this way? What if they don't want your damned colonial charity and your porcelain sinks and your air conditioning? She stared at him a long time. It was a cold, sickening stare. That was the point when things had started to slide.

He put her letter away in a box on the shelf. She was a damned good writer, he'd give her that. Still, she couldn't hold off nagging him even if she had to do it by mail. He was wasting his talents, she said. He should be with her in London or out at the front, following the Allies. No. He'd done enough of that in the last war. Front-line reportage was a game for younger men than him and there were plenty of good young men out there doing that job. He'd paid for his stint at the Italian front. He had a shattered kneecap and shrapnel wounds to prove it.

He went to his desk. One of the cats had peed against a leg of it. The cleaner had scrubbed at the matting that morning but he could still detect the sour fungal aroma beneath the bleach. The cleaner had muttered something about the cats, about how they were propagating beyond control, but he wasn't going to listen to that again. He wouldn't hear a word against the cats. They were his only company. They yowled and scrapped and fornicated with passing strays and made life in the villa bearable. He studied their politics, their hierarchies, their affairs. He allowed them to warm his bed and leave their furry cladding on his clothes and blankets. He had the dogs too and the fighting cocks and the staff and the makeshift crew of *Pilar*, but it was the cats he loved. The cats were his lifeline.

What did he care about the smell of cat piss? He probably didn't smell too good himself. His wife would have something to say about that too.

He had already completed his Christmas correspondence and his desk was bare. He couldn't think of anyone to write to. Apart from letters and the introduction for that war anthology, he hadn't written a damn thing since the last book came out. That was over three years ago. The same time he'd finally married Marty.

Three years since the Spanish Civil War book. The sales of *Bell* had stunned everyone, even himself. Scribner's reprinted and reprinted. Gary Cooper was the lead in the film. He liked Cooper. He was a decent shot and he knew how to grill a steak.

He should have won the Pulitzer for that book but it was stolen from him as he knew it would be. Some bastards couldn't bear for him to succeed. Still, he hated that stuff, the speeches and the posturing and everyone pretending to be his friend. He had always known that as soon as he won something he'd be shot to pieces as a writer. Sales were one thing. Clippings too. But win a damned prize and everyone is out to get you. Especially yourself. Better to be an also-ran and keep trying, pushing yourself on to the next thing and the next.

He took down a new box of pencils and tipped one out and started sharpening the end to a point. Clippings were rough. They ate away at you. If you were unlucky they ate away at your writing too. Even good reviews could be bad for you.

Setting you up for the fall. Well, he had taken the fall all right. But the last book was good, damned good, the best thing he'd done for years. The only thing, when he thought about it.

Now he needed to work. It had been too long and he was biting on the old nail and tasting the rust. He didn't have anything to pick up on, though he'd had some ideas about a Gulf Stream book. They had shriveled up on him. He needed to feel fitter to tackle that book. It would be a sprawler and he would need all his strength. He wasn't feeling too strong just now.

He went to the table and refilled his glass. He was breaking his rule about drinking and working but·what the hell? It was Christmas. He'd eaten his lunch without noticing what it was. Without caring. Sitting over the empty plates, he had thought about starting his memoir. Then he had put the thought in a glass of rum and drunk it off. He wasn't going to start on any damned memoir yet. He wasn't that dead.

He went back to the desk and shaped the pencil shavings into a pile. Then he flattened the pile and pinched the shavings into a line.

There was something though. What was it? Something he had just been thinking about. Not his wife. Not the Spanish Civil War book.

Clippings. He had been thinking about this lately: clippings could be a young writer's undoing.

Yes, he could use that. A young American writer sitting at the table of a cafe somewhere warm. Somewhere far from home. The South of France? Somewhere like Le Grau-du-Roi, where he and Fife had honeymooned. He saw him now, the young writer sitting at a cafe table, a pastis at his elbow, tearing open an envelope. No, slitting an envelope, with his wife's letter opener. That would be even better. The pastis is short and barely clouded by the iced water. The glass is very cold. The envelope is thick. The writer's first novel has just come out back home. He and his wife have been married a short while. They are honeymooning, just as he did. The young American writer's first novel is good, very good. The reviewers praise it. They praise the young writer's style. He is doing something new and brave. Everything is going along just fine for the young writer. Then the clippings come. His editor has forwarded them to him, with a note about reprinting. He opens the envelope and reads the clippings and the note. He is quietly pleased. He would like to celebrate but he doesn't want to make a fuss about it. He doesn't want to offend his wife. But why should the good reviews offend his wife? That is the problem. He is a promising young writer. The book is selling. The wife gets jealous. And the young writer's world begins to fall apart.

All because of the clippings.

How did it go from there?

He took another thumb of the rum. On top of the fishing and the sun the Cuban rum was another damned good reason for living here.

He should write down some of that stuff about the clippings. It might make a decent short story. But he didn't want to start in on it yet. He couldn't take it if he dried up before he even got started. He needed more to go on than the scene with the clippings. That would only take a handful of lines and the sketch would be done. He was a novelist now. Wasn't he? He couldn't pass himself off with those little vignettes anymore. He wasn't twenty-five. They would be after his blood if he tried that trick again.

He couldn't remember how it felt to be in the middle of something. It was so long since he had finished the last novel that all he could remember was the weight and drudge of the galley proofs and Max his editor sending him cables begging for more pages. The book went from proof to publication in three months. They were printing as he wrote. How had that felt? He couldn't remember.

He stretched and scooped the shavings into his hand and tipped them into the wastebasket. While he was at it he fetched the rum and topped up his glass a little. He took a good long pull of the rum and bent over the desk again.

His wife was the writer in the family now. She had squeezed out a novel between her bouts of boat- and plane-hopping, off to the sub war in the Caribbean, off to cover the Blitz in England. She was always off somewhere. What was wrong with Cuba? She liked the rum all right. They had a damned nice life here, thank you. She had fixed up the villa. The garden was coming on. They had the pool. The cook was pretty good. There was fine marlin fishing to be had in the summer and the boys loved it. It wasn't too much to expect her to be house-keeper now and then. Christ, was she his wife or not?

Probably not for much longer. That was it, too. Marriages coming apart. That could be in the story. He knew all about that topic. The young writer and his wife could row about the clippings. Maybe the young writer could take a lover and they could row about that. He could give that scene some ringside authenticity. He knew all about wives and lovers and wives and lovers being friends and everyone falling out about it. If only people could be happy playing at harems. He had tried that, loving two women who were friends and who got along fine, married to one and enjoying the other. But it didn't work, not for the women and not for him. Nobody realized how serious it was until it was too late. By then a man could be well and truly in love with both women and there was no going back and decisions had to be made one way or the other. He could certainly write about that.

He tested the point of the pencil with his thumb. It was sharp enough to leave a dent in the fleshy pad. He pressed it in again. Then he got the sharpener and smoothed it around the point a little more.

Lately he had been rowing with Marty as he had rowed with Fife when she found out about her. As he had rowed with Wicky when she found out about Fife. But there wasn't another woman to row about this time. Only the work that kept coming between them. Marty's work, not his. He had nothing to show for himself.

He was sick of women rowing. He was sick of bossy women. His wife was becoming like his mother. Christ, what a thought. His mother was sick back home, slipping in and out of a coma. He wasn't going back there. They could send all the cables they wanted. No way was he going back there again.

He poured another rum and went to the table to get more ice.

He had been brewing on the Gulf Stream story when he was out at sea on *Pilar*. Maybe that would come back if he gave it a chance. But what chance would he have in this state? He needed support. He wasn't going to get that any time soon. Maybe he did need a change of scene. If a story wasn't going to come to him then he would need to get off his ass and get out of the villa and find himself a damned story. Forget the Gulf book for now. He had already had that thought. Forget it. Maybe he could start a story about a writer's failed marriage. Breaking up with another wife was as good a time as any to write that story. The last book had finished off his second wife. He could use a book to help him through losing this one.

What he needed was fresh material. If he could go to the war looking for ideas that would be something. He didn't need to risk his neck as a reporter. He could gather what he needed for a great post-war novel. That was the real trouble. The last war made the lost generation and there was plenty to say about that. He'd said it in his first novel. What would this war leave? And who would have anything to say about it?

He would. He could command the field. His friends from the old days were all gone. Scott was gone, dead on the floor of a Hollywood living room, his heart wasted, cutting out on him. Joyce was gone, half-blind, half-mad, chipping away at the great dung heap of *Finnegans Wake* until his ulcer burst and did for him. The old heroes too. Sherwood Anderson, who he had loved and rejected and harpooned but never forgotten. Frail Yeats, surgically resurrected and banging a volley of young admirers, finally giving out in a hotel room somewhere on the Riviera. Even that wheezing old phony Ford had rolled over, though that was no great loss to him or to literature. All those old bastards gone and still here he was, still with work to do. He had outlasted them all. Outgrown them all.

What would come next? Across the water the mood was changing. It was all swing and GIs and young girls giving away their hearts to sailors. Flying the flag. So he'd heard, anyway. The last time he was in New York he'd been buried under those galley proofs.

He needed something vast. He needed something new and vital. The first novel had come out of Europe after a war. Maybe the next one needed to do the same.

All right then. He'd do it. He would cable his wife. No, he would write a letter, make her wait. He would take a front-line correspondent job and get back into his prose that way. He could go to London and gather ideas there. He wasn't doing any damned good here with his sub searches going cold and his brain shriveled up.

No need for Marty to win though. He would do it but do it grudgingly. She could think she had gotten him back into journalism where he ought to be, but she would pay for it. He would take her job at *Collier's*. He would tell her it was costing him a novel, taking him away from his Gulf Stream book. No need for her to congratulate herself on that. Even she wanted him to write another book.

He put the pencil and the sharpener in the drawer. He had the young writer and his clippings to work with now and he'd get started on it when he was ready. He'd think it over some more. He knew there was something in it.

He drank off his rum. Christ, he missed his wife. When she came back to Cuba he would give her hell.

How does it sound in your head? There is the voice, telling you how to look, to walk, to sit. You have no choice but to listen.

You are made to fit a role. Do not question what he has given you. He, David, Ernest, has the talent. You have the money. You accept this as you would accept having red hair instead of blond or black or brown, or eyes of two different colors. What is that called? There is a word for it. He has not given you the word, does not remember it.

You have other words, plenty of them. You have a talent for talking but you do not share his talent for drinking. Sometimes your words become tangled and you cannot comb them out. And so he, David, Ernest sends you off to bed. You make siesta and sometimes as you begin to fall into sleep he is there too, touching you lightly under the sheet. Ernest reaching out through David reaching out his hand. Or he comes stepping softly, barefoot on the carpet, over to the dresser for a book and leaving you to sleep, falling into that thick grayness as the door clicks behind him. He leaves you; he, David, Ernest, carries on without you, goes downstairs to read or takes the car into town or walks to the cafe to study the racing papers. Who knows what he is doing, he, David, Ernest, when you are not there? You hover. You float, suspended. Pieces of you are missing because he does not need you to be whole.

Heterochromia. You remember now. He remembers. He gives you that.

Your purpose is to serve him, David, Ernest, each in his way. There is a pleasurable neatness to this, a symmetrical quality. You are not a muse; do not assume that much. But you make his work possible. You are a bank account and a beautiful face and a source of recreation.

Is that enough? Isn't it?

Siesta is over. The afternoon sun is hard behind the blinds. You remember now. You remember that much of what you know is still to come, a foreshadowing. It is confusing, dreamlike. There is something about you that will change and things will happen that you already know. You know them dimly. Get up slowly. Rest in the chair by the bed.

You remember the moments before sleep. You remember the shape of David inside you, the wet slick of him on your thigh, on the sheet beneath you. Before that, before sleep and waking and rising and standing before the mirror, you had lunch together. You ate sea bass and drank some wine. It was a good lunch. David was happy. He had been fishing. You remember that. You remember him with the fish on the line and how you ran down to see him land the fish, walking it up the canal, the line bending with the weight of the fish until it touched the water. You remember sitting at the desk, this desk here. You looked through the window and saw him in the street below and you called out to him. What did you say?

You asked him to wait. That's right. What did your voice sound like? You are unsure. Should you test it again? Try it out? Can you even speak? Of course you can. You know this. But you have no memory of speech, of saying anything before that call. It was a plea, a cry of attention. But every voice starts this way. I am here. Here I am. Wait for me.

Well, here you are. What now?

2.

It has been three weeks. All good things in threes. After the shuffling of feet and springing hinges of seats Pen stands in the silent lecture theatre, waiting to hear herself speak. 'The Rule of Three in Modernist Literature'. Max O'Grady, not present, ever-present, lingers in the tiny green eye of the digital recorder on the desk. It is his ear, smooth and passive, open only for her. When the hour is over it will be gone, delivered by pocket or bag to the hands of Max, who will press it with his thumb and bring her back to life. He will sit at his desk surrounded by books and hear her, siren, summoning Joyce and Stein. He will lay back on the heaped pillows of his narrow student bed in his narrow student digs, notebook open upon chest, chewing the end of his pen, listening. Her voice in his room. Her voice in his world, and he listening to it. She looks at the metallic tube, longs to touch. But she does not. She does not need to. It will contain her voice, and that is enough. She tries to focus on the lecture. She tries to avoid the tiny green eye on the desk.

Then the hour is gone and the green eye is gone and she is a fraud of Gatsbyian proportions, standing on the mooring deck, staring her hopeless longing out to sea. She leaves the lecture hall and enters the rain, oh, ever the rain, and repeats the pattern. Office, emails, coffee, sandwich. Lecture, lecture and repeat. She must escape. But not yet. First there are tutorials.

She thinks: I was not made for this, was never made for this. She sees herself standing in the tide of Toby's old school playground, small boys breaking in waves against waiting mothers. She would narrow her eyes and seek out her child but she would never spot Toby: he would find her, tug at her fingers, surprise her with the colour of his hair or the cup of his chin. Other children found her too, sought her out in play centre or swimming pool. The sorry ones: girls with orange earwax under their curls, boys with oversized trousers and too-tight shirts, dirty-nosed, desperate for love. She thinks: Oh, shabby Madonna, wanting to give but never knowing how.

Pen reads the tutorial list: Jenny Galt, serial seminar skipper; Tom Bentley, one of four Toms in two classes (which? check his photo); Annabelle Patten, face rapidly hardening at the edges, eyeliner smeary as a faded tattoo. Pen suspects drugs. It is the same, she thinks, this pastoral business. A shepherd I shall not want. Other people's children. How much to care? How much to interfere? She lacks the essential coating for the job; once warmed, she oozes.

Not with Max O'Grady though. Not, not. She straightens in her chair. Emails scull past. Yet another Coleridge conference, Reading this time. A circular from Housekeeping about persistent damage to interactive whiteboards. She scans, deletes, archives. Max O'Grady. Half her age; *how now my calf.* She does the maths: Woody Allen and Mariel Hemingway in *Manhattan*.

She thinks: That second-year lecture on Hemingway.

The White Elephants in the room. The distant White Elephants. Something about spaciousness and claustrophobia, about intimacy and distance. She checks her online calendar – next Wednesday. How? How did she forget? There is time. A narrow leaf of it. Why did she take it on? It was Steve Saunders' class. But Steve Saunders despises Hemingway, teaches him through gritted teeth, calls him an illiterate thug. At the last faculty meeting she had waded in and defended Hemingway, called him the true voice of the twentieth century, said that whatever he did or said in life shouldn't, couldn't, cancel out the lessons of his writing. Why? Because of his sparseness. His leanness. The prose that revealed him as a teddy bear in a trilby, playing tough. A writer for the movie generation: the Brando of short fiction, beautiful but flawed. And, like Brando, fat and wheezing at the end, his prose a bloated imitation of itself.

She said it to spite Steve Saunders. She said it to say it. It was said. Now she must write the damned lecture.

The students come and go: Jenny with a fist of balled tissues and a note from Accommodation; Tom (the bright one – relief), right arm in plaster and a concession form. No sign of Annabelle. She logs out, rinses her mug, puts on her jacket. Applies lipstick. She will stop at the library on the way to the car. She will stare at some shelves, gather some thoughts about Hemingway.

On the library steps a student, lean and dark-haired, fights with the strap of an overstuffed red satchel. He looks up: Max O'Grady.

A hot bolt, a jolt to her stomach. She nods a greeting beneath her hood, sidesteps puddles, makes straight for her car.

Again in the rain. The rain colluding, detaining. Troubling.

She thinks: He is like a plant I have just learned the name of. Once unnoticed, now everywhere.

~

It is early, just past three, but she has escaped. She drives past the secondary school gates spitting wet teenagers onto path and road, perilous on weaving bicycles. She thinks again of Max O'Grady in the rain and she is him. She is him at fifteen, walking home from the bus, cars sloshing past, school trousers sticking slickly to the backs of his knees. Why go home? To what? Damp trainers steaming by the radiator in the hall. Four-page essay on irrigation. And tomorrow the fetid horrors of PE, interminable double Geography.

He is a boy. She thinks it, wills it. A boy, no more. No more.

She thinks: Toby could be half his age already. Thereabouts. Where is he from, this Max O'Grady? She knows nothing about him. She has shunned the lure of online student records. From where did he spring? Of what place? Was his a life of choices?

A trio of uniformed girls tangle beneath an umbrella, lighting cigarettes. She herself had no choice, no tests, no streaming: mainstream comprehensive, French classes an exercise in the impossibly exotic. Who from such a place could imagine Paris? Imagine, Paris! Playing shops like primary school kids, empty cereal packets furnishing translation time: *farine, blé complet. Je voudrais un croissant, s'il vous plaît*. The smell of glue like fish paste. Sharon Woods, pixie-eared and flat-chested, coming to class with her head shaved and Mrs Sayles telling them that the French sheared the hair of women collaborators. A mark of shame. The boys laughing, saying Sharon had lice, that they wouldn't have her if she begged for it. How she pretended like the other girls that Sharon looked ridiculous, and yet how breathlessly beautiful! Sitting behind Sharon in class longing to reach forward, to stroke the shorn turf of her neck, sleek as a seal pup. From which she wondered if she, Pen, was gay after all.

Until Michael Black from the lower sixth cornered her in the library and pushed his tongue into her mouth, her head shoved between the atlases on the oversized books shelf, and after the disgust, the wet mollusc of his kiss, spent weeks praying that he would do it again. Which he never did.

Oh, the rain. *The rain makes us reckless as rats.* The sun behind it is thin, watery, hibernal. She might believe in it briefly. She might trust in the sun, settler of scores, and she a grasshopper again. She thinks of walled pub gardens, glasses of crushed ice and mint. But the summer is gone, gone. The world has begun to ripen and rot.

Pen stops at the supermarket. Spider shapes and swooping bats swinging from ceiling wires. Halloween soon, harbinger of half-term, of Reading Week: a week without teaching. She picks up cat food, pizza, puritan conscience pricking, marking herself down against the eternal scorecard of duties done. And what? Why does it eat at her so, this falling below impossible standards? Nate never complains. She thinks: What if he did? A relief, perhaps. She could tell him to make the dinner himself if he didn't like it, to come home in time to make it, to come home at all, to be there, to be honest about where he has been for once, to do something. They could throw plates at each other. Never, not ever. Not Nate.

Rocket salad, low-fat yogurt. The drinks aisle, bottles towering, wine beers spirits. She thinks: The green light blinking, and no cup in hand. A glass of the green fairy. That way madness lies. Pulls out a bottle of Pinot Grigio – a safe pass, a token, but something, something, please let her. She is overthinking again: knows it.

Pen thinks: Max is in the corner of a student bar somewhere, lining up the happy-hour shots. As she would have done. Double vodkas and a scrounged roll-up. A game of pool. She hasn't played pool for fifteen years, more maybe.

She lingers by the freezer section, eyes scanning barcodes on the shelves. She should get home for Toby. She should get blindly drunk. She should look into Max's grades, check for a history of depression. She should leave well alone. She sees Max, hair dripping long into his collar, rain sliding inside. She reaches forward to touch it, tuck it behind his ear, feel the swell of lobe between finger and thumb.

Pen queues, fills canvas bags, drives home. Thinks again of Sharon Woods: seeing her on a visit home from college, all of nineteen, pushing a buggy with a child in it, two years old, more maybe. Hair grown out, home perm, a fold appearing above her left eyebrow; how she felt sorry, and relieved, and smugly satisfied. How Sharon looked at her, looked through her. No glimmer of recognition. She knew why: other girls hated her, bullied her. They had seen how life would be carved up.

She pulls up outside the house, rare, rare serendipity of parking spaces. Sharon's child would be Max's age by now. Older even. The house is dark, windows grey with rain: yes, Thursday. Toby has an after-school club – chess? Clarinet lessons? *Swimming.* Thursday = swimming. Jack Matthews' mother will drive him home. A plunging relief, a creeping shame. She knew there was something in the new school routine: she has not lost all sense, oh shabby, shabby Madonna. She unpacks the groceries, feeds the cat, gets out the laptop. She will log in, look up Max's student profile. It is simple concern. She makes tea, looks for milk, eyes the Pinot Grigio, slides it back into the fridge. Makes an orange dressing for the rocket salad, hopes for interruption. Does what she knows she should not: looks long and hard at Max O'Grady's student photo, a blur of hair and adolescent beard, now shorn, seeking his eyes. He is underwater. She sees herself reach forward, grasp the back of his neck, pull him up out into the air and say *I am here, I am here.* She presses an oversized fingertip to his lips.

The front door thumps open: Toby. She takes a last look, logs out, goes to her boy: damp-haired, long-limbed, increasingly, frighteningly mannish. Wraps herself around him in the hall-way. He hangs in her arms, a wet rag.

Are you all right? he asks.

Of course, she says. It's just an ambush. How else do I get a hug? How was school?

He shrugs. His stomach rumbles. She gets up, avoids his eyes, tells him to get his shoes off, get dry, get warm. She will fetch him a drink, a snack. She goes into the kitchen, opens the fridge door, leans in.

No, she breathes, to the salad drawer, to the milk bottles. No no no no.

~

Pen gives the Hemingway lecture. She says what needs to be said about the writer's brevity, about ambiguity, about famous last words. I'm fine, says the American girl at the end of 'Hills Like White Elephants', smiling in the face of betrayal. I'm fine. Let's get the drinks in.

Afterwards a handful of students cluster at the front. Pen presses buttons, tender, gathers notes, closes screens. Answers questions about essay deadlines. At the door she looks back to check the desk for stray papers, lost property, unloved keys.

Turning to leave, a hand holds the door open. She mutters thanks. She sees whose hand.

Max O'Grady. Taller than before, head and shoulders above her. She feels miniature, girlish, mousey. Silly. She swallows hard.

That was great, Max says. I hope you don't mind me sitting in. I know it's a second-year lecture but my friend told me you were doing it and I made such a hash of my Hemingway essay this term.

She says this is fine. She says she hadn't noticed he was there. She thinks: Thank God I didn't see you.

I liked what you said about Hemingway's women, Max says. I mean, that you find them sympathetic. I thought women wouldn't like his writing. I mean, you know, how he writes about women.

Pen thinks: He sounds anxious. Is he anxious? She thinks: Me, making Max O'Grady anxious? They walk together along corridors, Max opening doors. Gracious gallant youth. So attentive he might offer to carry her bags. She thinks: I could hold out my hand. Imperious. He might kiss it.

Have you read much Hemingway? Pen asks.

Not much outside the set reading, he says. More of the short stories. And *The Sun Also Rises*. I really got into that.

She nods. I loved that novel at college too, she says. Flinches. I still do, she adds.

Max waves absently to a passing girl, pink hair, armful of books. As the corridor narrows he leans in, elbow brushing Pen's back. She breathes, bristles.

My English teacher back home said that the best way to learn about a writer was to read their first work, and then their last, he says. Then fill in the gaps as you go along.

That's an interesting approach, I suppose, says Pen. So what do you make of *The Garden of Eden*?

They reach the college steps. Max stops.

I haven't read it yet, he says. Is that his last novel? I thought it was an African story.

Like many posthumous publications, she says, it's unclear how much of the African book is the author's work and how much has been patched in. Hemingway's son Patrick did a lot of work on the manuscript, published it to coincide with Hemingway's centenary. It felt gimmicky, like everyone was trying to cash in.

The wind picks up. She winces at the didactic ring in her voice, the list of responses. List, list and listless, like an android reeling off facts. She needs to get back to the office. She needs to pee: after so many years lectures still make her a little nerv ous. Max makes her more than a little nervous. He leans against the wall, leather jacket creaking, clearly in no hurry to leave.

So which would you say is his last novel? Max asks.

She is safe now. This is the ploughed trough of comfort and she can speak without a shadow beneath each sentence. She tells him of *The Old Man and the Sea*, the last novel, short though it was, published in Hemingway's lifetime. She tells him of *Islands in the Stream*, a posthumous novel of parts. She tells him of Hemingway's African manuscript, a jumble of memoir and fiction, edited into book form. She wants to say that there is something more to *The Garden of Eden*, something beyond the stripping back of a dead writer's clutter, something with integrity. She wants to tell him of the day she found her copy, twenty years ago, in a paperback sale bin on the South Bank, walking along the river with her married lover that nobody knew about, that she has never told anyone about, not even Nate.

Pen does not say this. Instead she tells Max that *The Garden of Eden* is worth reading, however it was published, because despite the editor trimming and revising it to make something saleable the prose still rings with that Hemingway clarity.

I should get a copy, Max says, shifting against the wall. Will they have it in the library?

Oh yes, Pen says, I would expect so. I think you'll enjoy it, she says. There's something about it that reminds me of *The Sun Also Rises*, which can't be bad.

She doesn't mention that the something is sex.

~

At ten o'clock that evening, Toby in bed, Nate at some after-dinner reception that bored him to speak of, Pen remembers the department planning meeting in the morning, thinks through all the papers. She opens her email to check for last-minute room changes: too many of these lately, senior management wading in, rescheduling timings. As she is about to log off a new message appears: Max O'Grady.

Thanks for our chat. I got the Hemingway book and am just about to start reading. Would it be okay to talk to you again sometime, after Reading Week? I know you are busy but I would really appreciate it. M x

M x. A kiss, or an elliptic a?

Pen switches off the laptop, rummages on the study shelves and finds it, tatty Grafton paperback, moody Lee Miller on the front cover, HIS FINAL NOVEL flashed in red across the bottom corner.

Careful, she tells herself. Careful now.

~

The room is tiny, a cell, cluttered bookshelves by the single window, a laptop on the desk. Empty bottles in the corner. The bed small and narrow, institutional.

Max's body is slight, elongated, his gangling gait gone as he lies on his side. Long-limbed, smooth, his body carved from the single trunk of a supple tree, his chest and belly taut and hard and wooden, his arms stripped sapling, his cock branching from the centre of his body, arching from root to tip, the end pressing against his belly. Against Pen's belly. She finds his mouth. Penelope, he says His hands in her hair, on her hips, lips fierce, tongue hungry. An alarm sounds, the hooting of a car outside, a passing ambulance, but it doesn't stop and he pulls away, looks at her, lower lip twitching slightly. The alarm cuts through and Pen slips away from the body and the bed and into her own, two darkened windows at the foot of the bed, the sidelamp on, her hair damp, a book open on her chest, Nate climbing in beside her.

Next door's bloody burglar alarm again, he murmurs.

She sits up, dry-throated, head reeling. The book slides onto the bed between them. She thinks: Dreaming. I was dreaming. I didn't really touch him. I didn't. He didn't.

She reaches for the glass of water by the bed, drinks deep, gasping.

Are you all right? Nate asks.

Weird dream, she says.

Weird good, or weird bad?

Debatable, she says. Her hand shakes a little.

Nate picks up the closed book, passes it to her. You lost your place, he says.

She puts down the glass and the book, turns out the light. Nate lays beside her.

You're practically panting, he says, edging away. Are you getting a fever?

I'm all right, she says. Just that dream. Goodnight.

Goodnight and goodnight and goodnight. She thinks: I didn't. We. Not. Max. I. Penelope.

She screws her eyes shut, forces her breath to slow, to still. Pictures a velvet vortex and plunges in, hopeful, wide open with longing.

Look at yourself. Look long and hard at yourself. Stand at the long mirror of the hotel bedroom. Your feet settle into the soft carpet fibers. It is a good hotel. You can afford it. Stay here, you say to David. Let us stay here through the summer. Let us keep on, on and on. Let us never go back to the world. Let us never be like the others.

It is a good speech. He, Ernest, is pleased with it. David agrees. You linger in front of the mirror. Stand there and look at yourself. Your calves and thighs are sculpted by walking and swimming and riding the bicycle in the hills. Your hips are slender. You look hard at these hips, the hips he, Ernest, gave you. Somehow they do not seem to be your hips. How could that be? You are entirely as he made you. And yet as you look at those hips, the narrow angles, the shallow pelvic bone, you know something is wrong. These are borrowed hips. They are the ideas of hips.

Do not be discomforted. Look instead at your narrow waist. This is good. This pleases you. Your belly is flat and your navel is a perfect disc. A disc. You peer at it, probe it. Is that right? Is that how a navel should be? There is a word for this too. Omphalic. He is pleased you know this word, Ernest; pleased he knows it to give you. You touch the dip of your navel and recoil. It is as if there never was an umbilical cord, never a wrinkling and unraveling and pinching and snipping and shriveling.

Do not dwell on this. Your breasts are small and high. Your shoulders are strong yet soft and round and your arms are supple. Your neck is smooth and narrow. Your hands are small and neat. There is a ring on one finger. Your face is oval, your skin golden, so smooth you cannot make out a single pore. There are no blemishes, no scars. No identifiable marks. Your hair is a heavy tawny curtain. Brush it out, away from you. Run fingers through it, feel its weight.

~

He watches you do this, he, David, Ernest. He watches your hair and you feel it coursing through you, his watching, his wanting. So this is what he likes best. Have you noticed it before? No, you haven't: but now you think about it there has never been a point that you noticed your hair like this. He likes it, David, Ernest. Would he like you if your hair was not like this? Would he let you change? Would he make you change it back?

You could try it and see.

Watch him watching you in the mirror. Dress yourself. Let him, David, Ernest, watch you dress. Let him watch you brush out your hair. Give him this one memory. It is a small gift. It pleases you to give it to him.

Pull on your rope-soled shoes. Say goodbye. Kiss him, David, quickly. Let him watch you mount the bicycle and cycle on through the village to take the road along the canal and into town.

You are gone. You have left the page. He, Ernest, knows what you are up to. He, David, has no idea. When you come back to him, David, the changes will have begun.

You cannot be sure what, but you know it is the beginning of something new.

1946: Cuba

It was one hell of a way to start another marriage. When he first met her in the bombed-out shell of London she was soft as a cat in her white sweater. His Kitten. His Kittner. He'd told her straight away that he wanted to marry her and that he hoped some day she would want to marry him. Never mind that he was still married to Marty. Never mind that Kittner was married too and had a pair of lovers bickering over her. A writer and a colonel. Well, he was a writer and a fighter both and they could take their chances. He knew what he wanted when he saw it. He always knew how to get it too.

He should have been writing but he had woken early and tried to write and nothing had come. And so instead of waiting in the house for Kittner to find him he went out to the garden and on through the gate and away from the villa into town. It was rare for him to make this walk but he needed it. He would stop at the bar and then walk back. He could spare this much of the morning and still get some work done.

They'd had their spats but he loved Kittner all right. He had brought her to Cuba and divorced his absentee journalist wife and they settled down a little together. He had work to do and she had the house and the garden. She couldn't expect to keep up her own work. He had learned that much from being with Marty. He was the writer in the house this time and he wasn't having his Kitten chasing newspaper work around the world. He wanted a wife that was like his first angel wife Wicky, or like

43

Fife, and would stick around and maybe give him the daughter the others had failed to deliver.

She'd soon started complaining. She missed her work. She missed her friends. The house wasn't her house, it was his third wife's house full of his third wife's furniture and photographs. Even their dinner was served by his third wife's servants from his third wife's china and he expected her to eat with his third wife's bloody monogrammed knives and forks.

Then she had said she did not want to marry him. She told him on the day itself. The guests were in the next room. The car was waiting. He shouted and broke a couple of glasses. She cried and gave in and went with him for the short civil ceremony and signed her name next to his. He cursed her in the car all the way back to the villa and he got through the afternoon by drinking and making low remarks. He didn't hate her and he hoped very much that he never would sink to it. He'd seen what that kind of marriage looked like. But he left her to sleep alone that night. She had humiliated him.

He came to the bar. The place wasn't open yet but he knew the boy would serve him anyway. He was always served whatever time of day, so long as someone was there and the door was unlocked. He could hear the whine of a tuning radio inside and called his order through the bead curtain that hung in the doorway. The boy answered that the floor was wet but he would bring him what he wanted outside. He brushed off a table under the veranda and sat down. His chest was tight from the walk and he was glad to rest.

Now he and Kittner had been married for a couple of months and they were both used to the idea. They wrote each other a lot of notes. He did a lot of apologizing. He knew right away that this was more like a war than a marriage and that like any kind of skirmish he needed to establish the rules early on.

The boy brought out coffee and beer. He watched the boy's easy movements as he turned and went back into the bar. He could see the boy stepping around wet patches on the floor through the long strings of blue and green beads. The beads glinted in the morning light and he put his hand up to feel the weight of them as they moved against the breeze. It was already hot but the breeze was cool. Later it would be much hotter. The rains hadn't gotten started yet.

He tasted the coffee. It was bitter and black and it left a powdery ache in the roof of his mouth which he washed down with some of the beer. As he drank he watched the boy mopping the floor of the bar. A rumba was playing on the radio. The boy's mop swung back and forth. His hips moved with it. Every now and then the boy would stop and lean on his mop and listen to the music and tap his feet.

Yes, he should have been writing. He needed to work and if that meant getting away from Kittner then maybe he should get a hotel room or go out on *Pilar*. He needed to be clear about this at least. Nothing was to get in the way of the writing.

Now he was on his fourth marriage he knew how it would go. He would need distractions. She would too. This was something they were both good at. When they were first together it was fresh and there was that novelty that always brought a good appetite. They would need to keep things interesting if they were going to stay together. There were plenty of other fine women he could get interested in and he knew he could interest them too. He liked that kind of game. He wondered if Kittner would take lovers as she had with her last husband. That would happen if he didn't shape up. He wondered how he would feel about that.

He drank some more beer. How was it he was already thinking this way? It was always new and absolute and then just as finely and distinctly it was gone. Love. In love he was the dart and the needle tip of the dart. He was the flights and the target and there was nothing else, not a single other thing around him, because even the air he moved through was made of the same stuff as he was. He was a good enough shot the rest of the time but when things got that mixed up it was a different story.

He had loved his first angel wife and their son and then Fife moved in on him, and so he loved her and married her and had two boys by her. Then there was the excitement of taking a younger lover who lived outside the rules of marriage and children and followed the war as fearlessly as any man. When he was with that young fearless beauty nothing else had mattered in the world. Nothing. Well, that lost its shine too. He married Marty and fought with her and then here was another. This Kitten in her white sweater and in his hotel bed in London with the Blitz and then in Paris when they broke through. In Paris it was like a homecoming and a liberation, and everything was new and fresh yet old and loved as an old photograph is old and loved. He was the first one at the bar in the Ritz hotel after the Nazis and the cellar was still full of champagne. He'd been at that bar with Scott, and with Fife and her rich uncle, and with plenty of other people that mattered a lot less. Then he was there with his new lover, and it was as if all those things that had happened only mattered because now he was there with her. He took Kittner through the streets he had walked with both of his first two wives and he was the same but altered. He felt swollen. His body was wider and stronger but there was a different feeling too. It was the feeling of a young man visiting his boyhood school or of a soldier returning to see how small the home he has fought for really is. But Paris was large enough to contain him for a while. He had poured all his ardor into the vessel that had become this fourth marriage. And now the vessel was cracked and he wondered how long he had before he decided to break it completely.

The hell with that, he thought. The hell with cracked vessels and the hell with shitty metaphors. He called through to the boy with the mop for another beer.

His war book was becoming more than a single novel. He had spent a good while thinking about this and now he was certain. He wanted to write about the war as a trinity. There was the land war with its shells and artillery fire and the smell of corpses. That was a hungry war where soldiers were half-starved. In a land war you were so tired you could sleep anywhere. Usually that meant on the ground. But the ground was your enemy and so you embraced your enemy whenever you lay down to sleep. Land war made traitors out of everyone. Then there was the sea war. That was removed and cold and somehow clean and spectral. There was fire there and water of course but there was also depth. Sea war was about being surrounded. When you fought in a boat or a sub and you were hit you knew that you would die because the element that held you up would also claim you. That was the pact you made as a sailor. If it wasn't the enemy that killed you it would be the sea and if you did last in the sea for a while then it would be sharks or fatigue or just the lure of letting go and sinking down into the cold quiet away from war. Then there was the air war, which was the most godlike of all wars because no amount of augury could tell those below when it would strike. Air war was fire dropped from above, hitting soldiers and civilians with equal detachment. It would take out farms and camps and schoolrooms and hospitals and bridges. It would take out soldiers and their wives and their mothers and their children born and unborn. Air war was unconcerned with the fate of the scuttling creatures of the land or the floating round-bellied creatures of the sea. Everything was alike from the air, and so nothing was of any worth.

He had begun the writing in several places. It was a swarming stream of ideas that linked together, and he had no intention of plotting or planning it. The books were all one at the moment but he knew they would soon separate and form themselves distinctly like shifting continents. There was the stuff about war and the types of war. There was plenty there about fishing in the Gulf and about his boys, and about how it would be to have his boys alone without their mothers or any other women coming between them. There was the idea of losing his boys too, to accident or war, and the sheering numbness of a father's grief. He had used the way that working and drinking and being at sea would help to fill the days of grief, and how grieving is like holding a great lid over yourself, a solid dome that can be scratched and bumped against but never broken. There was much about Paris too, about his early days starting out and learning his craft. There was a good deal about poverty and about marriage and of course about love and getting it and losing it without noticing. When he looked hard at it he could see that what kept cutting through was the story of a young American writer and his apprenticeship and the women that loved him and his work or didn't love his work and so tried to destroy it. It was the story about loving more than one woman and of how you go on fooling yourself that one wife or lover can be the everything that you want, and that you try to be the everything for them, and that this will, as you know, never work.

Yes, that was the part he needed to go back on. He saw it now. He needed to get down that young writer and his wife before he wrote himself too far away and lost sight of them. Maybe they were not part of the war book at all. He would find that out by writing it.

He finished off his beer. Men and women and work. Original sin. We are all bitched from the start, he thought. Then you try to throw writing into the mix and wonder why nothing ever comes off like it should.

The beads moved and the boy stood in the doorway holding out another glass of beer. He took it and nodded thanks. The boy smiled. As he turned back toward the bar the boy's hips swung again. The music was still in his head. He danced through the beads and back into the cool of the bar. The beads rippled behind him.

He sipped the beer. The boy's hips reminded him of his second wife. Small and dark-haired and boyish.

The story of the young writer was also the story of his second honeymoon in the South of France. Fife had made a Catholic of him and with that marriage he wiped out his first wife. Wicky was never truly his wife if the Church said so and it did say and because he wanted Fife, he listened. When he married Fife he was making revisions. His first son was born out of wedlock. His adultery was regrettable fornication, nothing more. This was a true marriage. His first marriage was a sham.

He knew at the time what this made him. He tasted the lie

when he signed the papers. Wicky had loved him. He had loved her. He had never been happier than when he and she and their baby lay on the mattress on the floor of the apartment above the sawmill in Paris. Now he rarely saw any of his children. He was desperate for a daughter. He had left his wives and their boys and now here he was, two more wives along, wanting another child and all the time wondering how long he could stand it.

He looked across the street. A dog trotted along the gutter, stopping every few yards to sniff and urinate. A man on a bicycle passed the veranda, his cap pulled down low over his eyes. The wheels of the bicycle ticked. He noticed the rear tire was a little flat, splaying out against the cracked dirt. It was many years since he had ridden a bicycle. He had cycled in Paris and in Le Grau-du-Roi with Fife. He was a young man then, climbing the hard hills, lean and sweating in the noon sun. Fife had chased him on her bicycle too, her body small and taut and powerful. The muscles of her legs were tight and her belly was smooth and flat. And his. Not now. He had gained weight and as his chest had expanded his stomach had become loose and bloated. He looked down. He disgusted himself.

That would change. He would make himself fit. He had the pool and he would use it. He could get a bicycle again. He would change himself. He could do it as he had done it before. He would cut back on the drinking and lose some weight. He needed routine: early rising, work, exercise. He should take the boat out more. Fishing strengthened him. He would feel better for it and so would Kittner. She had said to him in a note that his performance in bed was mechanical. No one had accused him of that before. She was right too. He had lost interest and he couldn't disguise it. Especially then.

He needed new tactics. It wasn't that his wife didn't look good when she made an effort, and she was still young enough to look fine without trying much at all. She was open-minded too and she was deft at a good many things. He ought to give her more credit. She wanted things to be right. If he could change to please her and make things better then he was pretty sure she would too. He would win her over again. He knew what he would like to start with. She had an idea of it but they hadn't talked about it much yet. Maybe now was the time.

He had talked to Scott about this many years ago when Scott made enough sense to get drunk with and talk to. They put down several whiskey sours and some Bollinger and Scott started in on how good a certain woman he knew looked since she had gone platinum and shorn the hair right up to the nape of her neck. It was short all over and clipped tightly around the ears like a schoolboy's haircut and the back of her neck was completely bare. The woman was a lesbian and one of her admirers had her hair cut to match the woman and dyed it the same color. Scott said that the woman was so enamored by this walking mirror that the pair soon became inseparable lovers. Scott said that the sight of the two women's bare necks was better than anything you could see in a Parisian nightclub and that it must be wonderful to feel like you were practically fucking yourself, except for the fact that it meant having to fuck a man, which held no interest for him at all. They joked about Scott's manhood and how many men he had frightened off and when they stopped laughing about it, he told Scott about his first wife.

When they were first in Paris together Wicky's hair was long and his was short. She had cut hers and he'd begun to grow his. Soon his hair was almost as long as hers and this excited them both greatly. They talked about this experiment and spent a good deal of time comparing heads and wishing his hair would grow out more quickly. When they couldn't wait any longer she cut hers again so they could be the same. It was being the same that mattered most, he'd said. He didn't like to think so much about his having long hair, about how it felt when he got home and took his hat off and felt the hair long on the back of his neck and inside his collar.

Scott listened carefully and nodded. When neither of them had said anything for a while he had made some joke about Zelda, and Scott came back with an obscene line about Wicky's new husband and some idiot at the bar complained and Scott threatened to knock him down.

That was all he could remember of the rest of that evening.

He could talk to Kittner about this idea. He remembered how he'd felt when Fife bleached her dark hair to platinum. It was her birthday and her surprise present to him. She had been up in Paris and he had been in the south writing and trying to finish his book. She and the boy had been sick and had stayed away but when they came down to meet him she was changed. She had a white-gold bob and her skin was dark from the sun. Her eyes were fierce and knowing and when she looked at him like that he could hardly bear it, but still he had to wait until her uncle had gone and the boy was taken care of before he could get her to the hotel room. They had been married a little while then. Whenever she changed her hair it did something to him. She was the same but different. Kittner colored hers too but that had happened early on and he was used to it now. Maybe they should try something different. Maybe red. Not the spun straw kind that Marty had but something bolder.

Maybe he could try it for himself. There was nothing to stop him. He could dye his hair copper and see what his Kitten made of it. Marty had put copper rinses in her hair. He could always say he had used an old bottle of her shampoo by mistake.

He finished his beer and stretched. He put some coins in the saucer. The idea of seeing Kittner pleased him now. He could feel it pleasing him as he stood up and rested briefly against the table's edge. He could work tomorrow. He could write about what might become of a man who dyed his hair to match his wife's. What kind of a bum would do that?

He called *adios* through the beads and crossed the street. The heat came at him as he turned the corner and the sun rose in a white sheet from the ground where the trees parted. He blinked and crossed into the shade.

Scott had tried to put the business with the hair into a novel but he had never really understood it. He was one of the best barroom writers around but when it came to thinking through the things that mattered to himself he'd never pushed his work further than those early pieces. Scott was too worried about what everyone else thought to uncover himself. Well, the hair was his thing and not Scott's. He could use it. He wasn't afraid to use these things.

Scott had been the only writer that could touch him. But that last book was truly lousy. Sometimes the magic was still there but when you read one of Scott's stories you always knew what to expect. Well, not him. That sure as hell wasn't going to happen to him.

No. He would not be like that. He would not put off the writing until tomorrow and tomorrow and drink until there were no tomorrows left and all his talent was pissed up against the wall. He would go home and start on it straight away. He would get started on it and he would mark out the story of the young American writer and his wife honeymooning in Le Grau-du-Roi with their dangerous marriage and their jealousies and their bicycles and the world waiting to take them apart and make them see each other for what they were. God help them then. God help the writer's wife when she knew what it meant to be married to a writer that actually wanted to finish something instead of sitting around in a back street drinking beer before lunch.

As he walked he could feel the beer suspended inside him. It sloshed and shifted like ballast. Soon he would need to pee. He hoped he would make it home. Don't think about it, he told himself. Think about Le Grau-du-Roi and slender hips and stroking that white sweater and the feel of a woman combing out your long hair.

He took the small rise to the villa slowly and stood by the gate to get his breath. He was in very poor shape. The heat and the walk and his clothes pressed on his bladder. The susurrus of crickets sounded like a water fountain. He went into the house and cut straight unbuttoning to the bathroom and felt the sweet panic of an old man sighting a distant urinal. He shut the door and lifted the lid and let out a low moan of relief.

~

The house was quiet. There were small signs of industry in the kitchen and someone had been washing windows. A sponge and bucket lay drying in the yard. On a side table he found a note from Kittner saying she had gone out shopping and that the gardener would be back later to clip the bottom hedges. He looked across to the pool and watched the flat surface of the water and wondered how it would feel to swim now, the water warm and the heat a flat plane spreading over him.

No. He needed to write. He went up and stood at his desk and thought how it would feel to write like he used to, like his young American writer would need to do, starting at first light and knowing that the day had still not begun and that he could have the work and the day both. If he had stuck it out that morning instead of giving up and going in to town he might have had a solid start to the writing already. There would still have been time to drink beer and swim after the work.

That was how it was for him before. Writing then eating then exercise. He needed the old pattern and the hard discipline.

He picked up a pencil and started on a fresh page. He thought of the heat outside and the ticking of the passing bicycle. He thought of the pumping of Fife's calf muscles, her slim hips and her body rising and falling. He thought of riding the red hills of the Esterel and of the butterflies in summer, hundreds of them like snow on the lavender bushes, like cherry blossom, and how they would rise and whir in clouds and weave between the spokes of the bicycle when you disturbed the air around them. He thought of the hard pull of the climb above the bay and the sweat on his neck and back as he rode and the great plunging fall of the descent, the rush of cool pine-scented air from the speed and the flight of it, and of laughing and then remembering the gnats dancing in sudden patches and trying to keep your lips over your teeth but grinning anyway.

He thought how it would be if he could have anything, anything at all. And that what he would choose was a young wife he loved and who loved him and to feel the swelling promise of the books he had already written building his reputation, the fame slight and the drinking easy, the strength of youth and the whole promise of his prime to come. He thought that this feeling was happiness, was the cusp of it. What would make the best story of all would be to take the man who has these things and watch him destroy them, slowly and surely, and see how he takes the fall.

He started to write. He began with the bicycle and the climb and the view of the sea as it spread out to Cannes. He put his young American writer there and made him climb the hill and then carry the bicycle down to the beach. The young writer sat on the rocks of a small cove where he often went to swim with his wife. This day his wife was not there. The young writer and his wife had begun to come apart. First there were the clippings and then swiftly and certainly the writing came between them. As he wrote it he knew there was something more, something else weighing on the writer as he sat and looked at the sea. Or someone. Yes: someone else would become like the writing and separate them. This would be the real turning point.

A noise came from the yard. He looked up. He wondered if it was Kittner coming back with her shopping. He heard the footsteps but they were not hers. They were the heavy tread of a man carrying something and he realized it was the gardener, coming to trim the hedges, perhaps pushing a wheelbarrow. The gardener would not disturb him or come into the house. The footsteps led away across the garden and softened as they reached the path. He turned back to the page again.

He had written this story before. It was a short story and a good one but no one had taken much notice of it at the time. It was the story of a bartender watching a young couple coming apart and of how the woman was leaving the man to be with another woman. The man could not stand it but he could not argue against the woman's logic either. He was not threatened like he would be if the woman had taken another man as her lover. He was jealous but he also knew it made no sense to be jealous of another woman. But there was more to it than that. He knew that somehow he was curious too and that he would let the woman go and that she would come back and tell him all about it, about what it was like when two women came together, and he would be inside it and outside it. The man in the story had tried to please the woman in ways that were not prescribed for men and women and he wondered as he sat there at the bar if this showed his true inadequacy. None of these things were written clearly in the story. It was a story you had to come to obliquely. Some of the story belonged to the bartender and some to the husband. Some of it belonged to the woman and her quick happiness and the ease of her leaving to betray the man with another lover, and the lightness of her step as she walked away. These were things he could use again. There was more to be said and he knew better now how to go about saying it.

The young writer's wife would take a lover. It would not be another man but another woman, dark-haired and lovely and the opposite of herself. The writer would feel the things of that bar story but this time they would go further. The other woman would fall in love with the writer. The writer would want both women. He would sit on the beach of the cove with his bicycle and his story forming beautifully and after a morning's work, after a hard ride through the pines, he would listen to the sea and he would miss both of his women, his wheat-haired wife and their shared dark lover. He would want both women and they would want him and each other and then it would get mixed up. It wouldn't take long for the wife to become the jealous one. And then the writer would be in love with two women at once and trying to work and finding that there was nothing a man could do to write his way out of that.

He would not get the easy money for a book like that but he was through with easy money. He had a reputation and he needed to keep it. They would notice later even if they didn't like it now. It was hard enough staying above water when the critics wanted you to sink, and he knew he could make it easier for himself and write something that would please everyone. But he would only hate himself. Some things were not written to be loved or even to be read.

This would be a different kind of book. He would write it as he had written those stories that the reader had to live through and work with. He would make it like the story of the woman leaving the man in the bar to be with her lover or the one about the woman needing and not wanting an abortion. Stories like that revealed themselves slowly. He would cut into the big war book and take what he needed to make a novel about the American writer and he would let it grow as it needed to, in patches and at odd lengths. Then he would trim it into shape when there was enough to work with.

He thought about this as he left the desk and walked through to the bathroom. He looked hard in the mirror. His beard was rough and his skin was patched with red. There were brown spots under his eyes and his eyelids were heavy and swollen.

Still, his hair was thick enough. It was short at the sides and longer on top. He pushed his hand through it. The cupboard under the sink was full of bottles and pots with old creams in. The lids were dusty and the writing on some of the bottles was faded and the labels wrinkled where they had gotten wet and been left to dry. He knelt by the sink and sorted through them. He found a large cut-glass jar of bath crystals that should have smelled like violets but let out the low odor of stale bread when he lifted the lid. Behind this was a bottle with a slick of thick brown liquid settled in the bottom. He turned the bottle over and righted it again. The brown sludge moved through the mass of clear liquid below it coating the sides of the bottle and sliding back to the bottom. He shook the bottle hard and watched the dirty color lift and swirl in the clear thin liquid and mix to a pale rusty lotion. He opened the lid. It smelled of ammonia.

He poured a little into his hand and then wiped it off. It left a small stain like a birthmark on his palm. He rubbed soap into the stain and washed his hand. He took off his shirt and put a towel around his shoulders. He stood by the mirror and watched himself lift the bottle and apply the lotion. His hands rubbed through his hair. The lotion ran over his ears and dripped onto the towel. It seeped onto his forehead and trickled into his eyebrows. He wiped at his face with the towel. A dirty red streak like the muddy gash on a fallen child's knee ran across his cheekbone. He put the bottle down and wiped the lotion from his hands into his hair and combed through it with his fingers. His hair was covered now. He wasn't sure how long to leave it before he should rinse it off. He washed his hands and patted at his neck and cheek with the towel

He looked at himself in the mirror. His beard was patched with white. His hair was coated the colour of the red mud slicks that streamed down the slopes of the Esterel in the wet season.

He looked at himself in the mirror and wondered how he felt about it.

What a stupid thing to do, he thought. What an incredibly stupid damned thing to do.

You look in the mirror. It is a different mirror, wide, brightly lit. Behind you in the mirror a man, comb in hand, scissors, scissors so sharp and pointed they strike you with terror. Like the beak of some terrible bird. But you are safe. Relax. You came here by choice, didn't you? The man is serious. He frowns as he combs your hair. One side of your head is heavier than the other and you understand, as you watch the man with the comb, that he has already cut much of your hair away. He works steadily, combing, snipping. You can see the right side of your neck reflected in the mirror. Or is it the left? The hair there is short, cropped to show your earlobe. Now he works on the other side, snipping and combing, bringing the two halves together. He stands back, behind your head, tips you forward, spins the chair gently, adjusts and appraises. He turns the chair back and you look at yourself.

More, you say. Shorter.

Mademoiselle asked for an Eton crop, the man says. This is not an Eton crop, Mademoiselle.

Something bursts inside you. You do not like to be corrected: you find this out. It comes to you in a rush, this contempt. You will not be thwarted. Your fingers lace together in your lap.

There is a ring on your finger. It is Madame, you say. You hear the cold metal of your own voice.

You tell him how you want him to cut your hair and where. He does not speak. He does as you ask. You see the snarl of his mustache.

Contain yourself. Do not spoil this.

Look at yourself. There is something inside your eyes. You peer hard into the mirror and you see a shape moving in the shadow of your iris.

The first time, you come back to the hotel with a boy's haircut and it shocks David and delights him. It's not the only time and he doesn't always like it. But you are mixing things up. This happens to you. Do not trust chronology. What does chronology matter? It doesn't matter to him, David, Ernest. They are writers. It is their job to play with narrative time.

But still. It does happen. The changes are under way. This is what matters. And in the fishing village, in the streets and galleries of Madrid, in the winding roads around Biarritz, this is all that matters. Places make small differences to you, minute additions and adjustments. What changes is not the geography but the slow accumulation of yourself, of the small feelers of will that you stretch out.

Stretch them now. Feel the extremities of your fingers. Feel the solidity of bone beneath your scalp. You may doubt it at times, but here you are.

There are little things, trifles. They amount to nothing. Yet – yes. You sense them. When David is asleep. That is when you are meant to lie there too, passive, shut off. But it doesn't always happen. There are times when Ernest leaves the room, rises from his desk, walks through streets that appear around you, places you and David inhabit, and you follow him. Stranger still, he takes you to where nothing is familiar. Street signs you cannot read, dingy bars you would never step inside. You sit at the table with Ernest and he orders coffee, or beer, or rum, or schnapps, and he takes out his notebook. You watch him. Does he know you are with him? He must. Sometimes he stares at you, right at you, as if he were seeing you for the first time. Sometimes he smiles. What would happen if you spoke? Or reached out to touch him, rested your hand on his shoulder? He would feel it. Surely he would. Yet he looks at you as if you are not there, and when someone else comes over, joins you at the table, he never says your name or offers an introduction. As if you do not exist.

But you do exist. Don't you?

3.

Half-term. Reading Week for her students. Pen has some marking to do, oh ever the marking, but the days are clear. She has a pile of reading to digest. There is the Gertrude Stein book to chip at, that monolith blocking her view. She must embrace it, pace out the territory of those middle chapters, steady herself into the encircling work of it. She thinks: See it as a treat, luxuriating in a leather armchair, pots of tea, squares of sunlight on the carpet, notebook. The researcher's dream. Her week is free: Toby's football school starts tomorrow. Today he is at a loose end, fidgeting, listless. Moping around the house.

She is restless too. She has fallen deeply into *The Garden of Eden*, wandered in and left the gate open. She has abandoned the writer David Bourne with his pencils sharpened, his cahiers open. She is anxious for him, for his unformed story, for his envelope of clippings. She envies his life. She too wishes to wake in a hotel and make love before breakfast, eat brioche and soft buttered eggs in a cafe, drink cold wine on the beach and swim naked in a warm sea. She eyes the worn paperback cover, the woman's slight neck, the folded orange edge of train-ticket bookmark. She wants to climb back in. To dive deep, to steep, to soak. To abandon all others.

But today is rare. Today she has Toby to herself.

Pen sorts piles of laundry, loads a wash into the machine. So soon gone, irretrievable, the youth of a child, the endless months of preschool. Shapeless weeks punctuated by a few hours at playgroup, the odd babysitter. Never a page written, the books by the bedside piling unread. Blank slates of days that she filled with adventures for Toby: the zoo, the beach, libraries, museums, galleries, Nate always working, always travelling, always elsewhere. But the joy of possession, the gift of first experiences: Toby marvelling through train windows. Toby charging, head down, imaginary sword swinging, across the toothy walls of castle ruins. That fierce lioness love. She is seized by it again, by the desire to reclaim her child. Toby has entered the final throes before adolescence, already walking the corridors of his last school years, jostled by the elbows of teenage giants. He will be that giant soon. She has let so much slip away from her, uncherished.

She finds Toby cross-legged in the corner of his room, half-reading a magazine, picking detritus from his football boots. Little clumps of dried mud and matted grass on the carpet beside him. She thinks: Microhabitat. She thinks: The great turf. She thinks: What eleven-year-old boy spends the first day of half-term cleaning his boots?

The sun is shining, she says.

Toby looks towards the window. It's going to rain, he says.

Let's escape it, she says. Let's go. Time for an adventure.

Toby grins. Pen's throat flutters: he is still her boy.

She throws some things into a bag, checks the car for essentials: picnic rug, pocket macs, change for parking. Toby brings his magazine and rollerblades. Pen reaches for the Hemingway novel.

Is that for work? Toby asks.

Not really, she says.

Yes it is, he says. I can tell. Holiday rules, okay?

She leaves it on the table. Closes the gate on Le Grau-du-Roi: soft sensual beaches, bleached bays, salt bodies.

They climb into the car, Toby shifting and adjusting the passenger seat, still relishing the recent removal of the booster cushion. His legs long now, tapering tubes of frayed denim swallowing his trainers. His hair heavy on top, unbrushed. Pen takes him in, his candour, his serious mouth. Swells with the pride of ownership: she made this boy. He is beautiful.

Where to? she says.

Anywhere, he says. Frowns. Then adds: Not shops.

~

They drive to the coast. She is led by the absence of the book, the longing, the loosening yellowed pages. She wants a glass of dry white wine in a cafe overlooking the sea. She wants fishing boats and hard, wet sand. She wants David Bourne, to have him, to be him, young and certain and ambitious and with all the time his wife's money can buy. She wants his wife. She wants anything but what she has. She thinks: Except for Toby.

When they get out the sun has vanished. Pen shoulders the picnic rug. Toby raises an eyebrow, rolls his eyes at the clouds. She shrugs. They walk along the promenade, past the screaming jingles of arcades, the disconnected lights of the amusement park, the scaffold cladding. The sea is celebratory as grey icing on a birthday cake, the tide spread artlessly in the centre of the bay, missing the spongy edges. Mobs of gulls stalk the perimeter. Despite the October clouds the beach is littered with people: tribes of boys wrestling each other and digging holes, grandparents overseeing squabbles, camps of sandcastles, windbreaks, the odd squealing paddler braving thin waves. Pen finds a dry stretch of sand and rolls out the picnic rug. They sit in silence, muffled in fleeces, watching the sea inching in. The surface barely ripples yet the tide rises, the unfathomable weight of things to come slowly stealing closer. A party of women passes, bare feet, saris and cardigans, speaking – what? Urdu? Pen curses her ignorance, envies the otherness of it. To be so other, so elsewhere. To be Catherine Bourne, young, high-breasted, scandalous in sweater and slacks, walking the out-of-season sands.

Toby graciously feigns interest in Marmite sandwiches. Pen rubs sand from her jeans, squeezes his knee in gratitude. Offers the prospect of the gallery cafe later.

The rain spits. They finish the picnic, gather wrappers. Stand to roll up the rug and the rain begins in earnest, hard drops pitting the sand, pocking the surface. Plosive. The beach empties. They rustle into plastic raincoats, retreat to the harbour arm.

Inside the cafe they sit damply on perforated chairs, shivering. Hot chocolate and whipped cream by the huge grey windows; walls, tiles and sky the same wet marble slabs. The picnic rug on the seat beside them is incongruous as a lank, wet sheep.

They look around the exhibition. Toby slouches through the gallery space, unmoved, crumples into an ungainly heap on a bench. Pen notes the animal length of his limbs, the raw youth of him. She thinks: Soon he will tire of everything we do together. The blue figures on the walls all look the same to her. The seaside visit feels woefully misjudged. She flops onto the bench beside her son.

Tobe, she says, to the clipped hair of his neck, his pale left ear. Let's go bowling.

~

The week unravels, smooths itself into open hours that are all Pen's own. She portions out desk time, allotting an hour to emails and admin, three hours to the Stein book. She transcribes notes and fills in the manuscript, subsection by subsection. Dutiful. Stolid. A labour. The rest of the day is given guiltily to Hemingway, to reading and rereading *The Garden of Eden*. She devours, regurgitates, repeats. Chapter by chapter, passage by passage. It fills her head like infidelity.

She thinks: This is like being in love.

She thinks: He is doing this too. Max O'Grady, holding this book, reading these words.

She thinks: The poet that read the same book as his lover while they were apart. Words holding worlds together. Who was that? Verlaine? Reverdy? Not O'Hara. *My heart is in my pocket. It is poems.* Lives threaded together, real and imagined, punctured with the same needle. Reading as a conversation. They were in the book and beyond the book. The book was everywhere. Bound and unbounded.

David and Catherine on the beach. David and Catherine in bed, experimenting, transgressing, becoming other. What was Hemingway up to? Pen thinks: There is no judgement in this text. There is fantasy and role play and acceptance. There is danger and release. Then there is the argument over David's work.

When David closes himself away to write, his world is beyond Catherine's. Pen feels his retreat, the table by the window, the brass bedstead, muted sound of sea, senses closing, everything narrowing to a point, pressing the page. The hard clarity of first sentences. She envies him, his stillness and sureness. David writes about his childhood, his boyhood in Africa, his father. Love and hate and betrayal and nurture. But his wife is not of this world. Catherine cannot touch it. She has no access. She wants him to write about their lives together, a travelogue of their adventures. Does she stifle him? No. He is a writer. He is the seed of Hemingway's mind and between the pages of his lined schoolboy's notebooks he will do whatever the hell he likes. He carves out his own world. It is a conversation Catherine cannot join. Is she jealous? Is she mad? Is she simply a poor reader? She claims he is wasting his talents. Does she believe it? What does she want? To be his muse? Or his creation? She makes herself in his image. Eton haircuts that harden and shorten, fishermen's shirts softened with washing. Drinks his cocktails. Loves him so hungrily she tries to become him. Pen has endured this kind of love. It is absolute consumption, exhausting. She pities Catherine, feels for David, the weight of another's happiness pressing against his own, another's wants. Moulding, needing. And the frustration of not creating: of being always audience, never actor, however close, however involved. Catherine doesn't even get to play muse. And Pen? She thinks: How many lives ago did I last inspire a line? She thinks: I am the shirt on David's back. She thinks: The Stein book is a tribute, an obituary. It is not alive in itself. And me? And me?

Pen turns back to the end of Book Two: David and Catherine in Spain. There is remorse. David drinks absinthe. Absinthe tastes of remorse. Pen can taste it, can feel the bite of the glass against her teeth. There have been too many changes: Catherine into his Devil, into a boy, not only at night in the hotel bed where it is play and David can stand it, but in the day too. It is in the way Catherine walks and the way she observes him. It is in the way she looks at other women and at the pictures in the Prado. Now he cannot stand it. He goes to a cafe while Catherine takes a walk and he drinks down the green fairy of remorse and he is still drinking it when she comes back. Catherine feels his remorse and mourns it, becomes a girl again, sitting in the cafe, the fountains in the square behind her, the play of light proving it is real. Pen sees the fountains, hears the fall of water, the weight of it in the heavy air, the walls of the high buildings surrounding the square, the sound of soft summer shoes dusted with pollen and red earth, the green tinge of glass in the cafe windows. She is there with the American couple who are in love and falling apart, watching them as the waiter watches them, as Hemingway watches them, curious and a little anxious, a sickening sinking at their impending quarrel, hovering just out of reach. Catherine proud and alert to the danger and willing to be anything her husband wants and if he wants a girl then there she is. But there is bitterness in her change, resentment. David likes her as a girl. She is glad someone likes it because to her it is a goddamned bore and she will make a scene, a slight one, hysteria a proof of femininity, playing up to type. But Catherine will also hold it down, as David tells her to. She will hold it down in front of the waiter and the locals lunching in the cafe and betray nothing, reading her mail, another disappointed American tourist. Trapped in her own self. A woman, whether they like it or not.

Pen closes the book, looks up blinking into the room. She had forgotten this: to read and to be so far inside a world that to come up is to be thrown helplessly out, a hooked fish on the riverbank. Not only the leaving, the resenting of it: worse, she cannot remember how else to be.

She stands, goes into the kitchen, clicks on the kettle. Her knees buckle, her head swims.

She is amazed at herself, at finding herself standing there: the cafe gone, the couple gone, the waiter no longer lingering discreetly, polishing glasses at the bar. She sees her own kitchen as if from some vast distance, the cupboards lining the walls, the butcher's block in the corner pendulous with ladles, the clock above the sink. The window is dark, steamed up, a fog fenced by mobbing shapes of trees swaying in the garden.

She doesn't know herself. She doesn't want to know herself.

And yet she also senses the terrible clarity of things: sudden and resolute as if after fever. There are the milk bottles, rinsed and ready for the doorstep. So clear in their being that she sees black lines around them, their separateness absolute. The windowsill cluttered with keys and plant pots, a chipped jug for flowers. Every item clear and distinct. She thinks: That line in Joyce's *Ulysses. Ineluctable modality of the visible.* Physical. She thinks: Joyce always has it. Always.

She says: That is why we read. Says it out loud, to the mixer tap, the inverted globe of her face reflected spoon-like, pink and hideous. That is why we read. The world is too bloody real. It is more than she can bear.

She thinks: Reading and mental note-taking and analysis. Always reading as work, despite herself. How long has it been since she let herself read like this, as she is reading Hemingway and Catherine and David? Immersed, saturated? She has become an anatomist, a specimen collector. She had forgotten how a book can breathe.

She clenches fists, relaxes. The kettle thunders to a climax. Steam tickles, moistens, evaporates. And there it is again, the fizz and fall in her stomach, the trapdoor opening beneath her. She thinks: The body remembers, the body is quicker than the mind.

Falling for the impossible world of a book is one thing, a hopeless crush, a fantasy, quickly dispelled. Falling for Max O'Grady is another matter. She thinks: This is the first wave of danger. The true force of it. She thinks: Stop digging. Stop digging, and the damage will be slight. A few bruises. She rubs her wrist, watches the blush rise beneath her thumb. Her skin prickles. Too late, it says, too late.

Pen shakes herself, looks into the darkening window. Watches as the woman looking back slaps herself in the face: once, twice. Feels nothing.

Why is she standing there? She cannot recall. She goes upstairs, irons Toby's school shirts just for something to do with her hands, hangs them on the inside handle of his bedroom door and listens, desperate, wavering, to the depth of his miraculous untroubled sleep, the mound of his body rising and falling in the centre of the bed.

~

Sunday evening. Pen sweeps floors, fries eggs for butties, frilled lace edges curling, carbonating, spitting oil at her wrists. The rhythmic kicking of ball against back wall: Toby, bored, dreading the impending return to school, a Monday morning maths test. Pen had imagined things so other than this, so so other. Imagined a kitchen cluttered with copper pans, a range, a floury apron hanging, a wreath of onions. Imagined a study in the attic, conference papers, a shelf of critical works singing her name, a publisher driving down for the weekend, making an effort, eating her Sunday roast. Sitting up late drinking Rioja with friends, red circles on the scrubbed kitchen table, running candle wax. A lover who brought flowers, who enjoyed her ruthlessly against the furniture. Imagined, yes. Not this.

Nate is gone. Another night in a dormitory hotel, an early flight to catch. Or so he tells it. Pen thinks, inevitable thought, of Max O'Grady. She thinks: Am I jealous after all? Or just lonely? Is that why? She thinks: All this study and nothing learned. She thinks: So this is the life of the mind. A mind that needs mending.

She butters rolls, pours tea, gets Toby's ketchup from the fridge. A college friend once told her that Wittgenstein worked on his *Tractatus* while living in a shack, eating tins of baked beans, caring nothing for what he ate as long as it was always the same. The poet-philosopher made real. All of the clay. She had pictured Wittgenstein, wiry curls dampening, orange sauce clinging to the corners of his mouth, sweating out a hangover. Had that ever really been?

She thinks: Flightless birds. She thinks: I could write a thousand papers, but there will always be clothes on the line, leavings in the sink.

She calls Toby in to wash his hands, to sit, to eat. Checks his fingernails for filth. She could tell him this, she thinks; tell him the dirty secret of life. Suck the marrow of his innocence. It never really gets better, she wants to say. This time tomorrow your maths test will be over. But more will follow. She wants to say: There is only ever a different kind of dread.

She does not say these things. Instead she runs his bath and checks his revision, fractions, percentages, hangs out his uniform, kisses him goodnight and tells him that it is only a test and when it is over he will still be him and everything, everything, will be fine.

In bed, Nate's side a cold uninhabited territory, she revisits Hemingway's Eden, devours the pages, envious, resentful. Switches out the light and blinks dry-eyed into the darkness.

Fine. Just fine.

He is not looking: he, David, Ernest. Yet you are still here. There is the road, stretched out in front of you. How did you get here?

David?

David is at the hotel. Good. He is writing. He went to the room where he works and left you sleeping. So how did you come this far? What can you remember?

Pull over the car. Yes, now! Anywhere on this stretch. Yes, there.

Feel the steering wheel. Feel the engine ticking. Turn it off.

The train goes past, cutting through the hills. Watch it disappear. You have driven this route before. Why are you shaking? Are you shaking? It is nothing. You must be here for a reason.

Think. Think about why you are here. Did David hear you leave? Did he notice the sound of the engine? He was in his room. Perhaps that was it. David heard the sound of your engine cutting through his story and Ernest sent you off on a drive. There must be a motive. There is always a motive.

Concentrate. Why would you take this road? Where are you heading? Cannes. Of course. What for? David does not know. Ernest must know. He would not send you off without a reason. He would not leave you out here on the road if he wasn't going to bring you back.

So: think. Start the engine again. Turn the wheel. Drive on, up and over the rise and down to Cannes. It's a pleasant drive, isn't it? Feel the breeze on your neck. Feel the air on your forehead. Does that feel better?

Here is Cannes. Is this Cannes? Yes, it must be. There is the cafe you stopped at before. Pull up outside. Get your bearings.

You peer at the cafe. It is different. You remember the shape but it feels wrong somehow. There is the door. There are the trees. But the trees look fuzzy, indistinct. Peer at them. Are they clearer? Perhaps it is just your head. Perhaps your vision is affected; headaches can do that. But the cafe. Yes, you are right there. It feels abandoned. It is like a cafe in the desert. A mirage. It is like a cafe in a partially constructed film set in a back lot. Like a sketch on stretched canvas. Like you could walk over, walk behind it, knock it flat with your foot.

Breathe. Breathe. You are breathing, aren't you?

Yes, you are. Your chest rises and falls. There are pearls in a string around your neck. Touch them. Feel the hard roundness of the pearls. They are real. They move as you breathe. Your hand at your throat feeling the pearls. Feel the pulse in your neck as it bulges and retracts.

It troubles you. Do not get out of the car, then. If something is wrong it is better that you drive back. Perhaps you really are unwell. Turn the car around and head home, back to David. You will feel better when you see him. Seeing him makes you feel whole. That is as it should be. Isn't it?

You drive back and as you drive you feel fuller, heavier, denser. You are coming back together. The closer you get to him, David, Ernest, the more certain you become.

You pull into the passing place. Why are you stopping here? You do not know. But you do, because something has happened to you, something has clicked into place.

Ernest is not here. But you are. You still are.

1948-51: Venice Paris home

The Gritti Palace was the best hotel in Venice. It was the kind of address he enjoyed and the service was on a level with what you'd expect at the Ritz. The bar was well stocked and had a long marble counter that kept your drink cool. If you were lucky and the weather wasn't too hot and the water too foul you could sit at the terrace by the Grand Canal and look over at the palaces and the basilica of Santa Maria della Salute.

He had been lucky that day because it was December and so the air was cold and clear. He sat with his collar up and his hot coffee with the brandy in it and looked out over the canal. His fingers were cold but he held his pencil above the page of his notebook and thought hard about how he could write down what he had been thinking about since lunch. He needed to be alone but didn't want to be in the room upstairs that he had shared with Kittner. He needed to look at the basilica and the water of the canal and to think.

His wife had gone back to Cortina to sort out the house for the winter. He'd taken in plenty of duck hunting since the season started and had been up to a lodge above the city for some more shooting. It rained hard while the party were out after the birds and though this did not matter to him the owner of the lodge insisted that they go back and get dry. He followed his host with the rest of the party and once the guns were in they were invited for drinks by the big open fire in the lodge house.

By the fire was a girl with quick green eyes. She had been caught in the rain and her long black hair was wet. She was laughing and combing her hair and spreading it out over her shoulders to dry. Her nose was a perfect Venetian bridge of a nose, her bones fine and strong but her features delicate. He had seen many beautiful women that impressed him, but this time it was different and he could not keep his eyes off her.

That was two days ago. He was so struck by the Venetian girl he could barely speak to her. Instead he talked to his host and the men of the shooting party and made sure the girl could hear him. There was a young man with the girl who turned out to be her brother and another one who was a cousin of some sort. He found out the girl's name and where she lived and invited her and her brother out to lunch.

Now he and the girl had met and lunched and talked a good deal. He ate the food without tasting it though he'd chosen the veal and it looked and smelled delicious. He ordered champagne and kept the glasses busy. The girl was light and lively and she laughed and smiled at his stories and drank the champagne. The girl's brother was unable to come to lunch but he sent his sister with a friend as escort and a very formal note of apology. The escort was handsome in his way with a broad chin and long nose which he dipped into the champagne glass when he drank. He was charming and attentive to the girl but it was clear there was nothing between them.

After lunch he offered the girl and her escort drinks at the bar in the Gritti but they declined. The girl said that her mother expected her back at any moment. They walked to the door of the hotel together and said goodbye. He kissed the girl's hand as she left and he could feel the softness of her fingers in his and the touch of her skin on his lips. The girl's hands were so smooth and young that he felt repelled for her and disgusted by his mustache that was coarse and graying. The girl smiled when he kissed her and he looked up from her hand and into her eyes to see how she reacted. Her eyes were very wide and green and when he looked at her she lowered her lashes in the way some women do when they see something they want.

That was all the encouragement he needed. After he watched the girl walk away he went straight up to the bar in the hotel and ordered his coffee and brandy and sat on the terrace to think.

For the last two years he had been writing about the war from the land and sea and air and it had gotten out of hand. The manuscript was vast and as he tried to carve it into separate books he kept making other parts that didn't fit. He had shelved the story about the young American writer and his wife and their lover in the Riviera because that had grown too big as well. Everything was growing and swelling and getting out of reach.

He needed to write a war book. Everyone had expected him to do it. It was long overdue and people had begun to look at him like an artefact. Already biographers were running pieces on him. There was no surer way to kill a man's career than to write a biography about him. He needed to get a novel out straight away and so he'd been working on a piece of the big manuscript that was about the land war and some of the mistakes that had been made there. All the duck-shooting had given him an idea about how to shape it. An old colonel waited with his gun in a duck blind thinking about the war. It would be a bitter story. The colonel had been demoted and he felt washed up after the war and sour about the way he had been treated.

The Venetian girl had changed things. He knew he needed to have her in this story. She would be the love interest that brought out the parts about the war. The old colonel and the young Venetian beauty would talk and make love and their story would give the bigger war story a structure. That was how he could rewrite what he had and make it into a novel. He thought about this as he sat looking at the basilica and drinking his coffee and brandy but he was almost afraid to write any of it down. He felt like Dante on the Ponte Vecchio. The girl was too perfect and he feared she might disappear.

He went on to Cortina for Christmas with his wife and thought more about the story of the colonel. It had been hard trying to work without seeing the Venetian girl and he had black moods and rowed with Kittner. He bullied and railed and called her every name he'd called her before and some he'd kept in reserve. When it was like that he couldn't stand the sight of her and she knew why, so he made her pay for it with hard words and by drinking and sometimes using the back of his hand when it got rough. In the New Year he found an excuse to travel back to Venice for business and saw the girl again then. Her mother disapproved but he was immune to mothers. After that he was apart from the girl until the spring, when they came back to stay at the Gritti again.

Whenever Kittner went out sightseeing he would meet the girl and take her out for lunch or for drinks. He would tell her about his writing and his war exploits and she would listen. Then they would walk or take a gondola and he would look at her and she would laugh at his long looks to break them. In the afternoons they would sit in the spring sunshine in the squares and drink coffee and she would cross her long legs beneath the table and let their knees touch.

After that he and Kittner went home to the Finca Vigía. He had done some serious work on the colonel's story by then and he knew he had a novel. The writing went quickly and smoothly and he felt like a young man again, up in his tower room overlooking the harbor, writing the story and putting the eyes and hair and long slim hands of the Venetian girl in it.

He worked through the book from that summer to the winter and gave it to his publisher. He hoped to see the Venetian girl but that didn't happen. Months passed. He and Kittner went on to France and through to Italy again for the winter and still he did not see the girl. Finally he made it back to Venice for Christmas. It was a year since he had first seen the girl but he could still picture how she had looked by the fire in the lodge. When he saw her again in Venice he knew how he felt about it. He wasn't going to let her get away again. He invited her to come back to stay with them in the house in Cortina. There was nothing his wife could do about it. The girl agreed.

Kittner told him he was making a fool of himself. He didn't give a damn. So what if he was a fool? She was the kind of girl men became fools over. She was the kind men went to war over.

He had her with him in Paris too when the spring opened up and there were small fragile violets and yellow pads of primrose at the bases of the trees in the boulevards. She was young and slight and graceful. She was so beautiful and fresh that even in the streets of Paris where they are accustomed to beauty people stared at her when they passed. Men looked and admired her and women took in her loveliness and made what they could of it for themselves. She was taking art classes in Paris then and he was staying with Kittner at the Ritz. The girl's brother was away looking for work. Her family was an old family of great respectability but the money had dwindled with the invasion of Europe. Her father was dead and since the war was over the family had become straitened and their finances were in trouble.

He was established and his money was his own. He wasn't living off Kittner as he had been forced to do with his first two wives. He could help and protect the girl. She was young and poised to come fully into life and she needed someone to take care of her and nurture her through that difficult time. He called her *daughter* but they both knew, as his wife knew, that this did not cover everything he felt about her. He wanted to hold her and shield her from the bad things that would come to her in life. He also wanted to be the one to show her how things really were. At times he felt that this was a courtly love and he was a battle-scarred knight worshipping her in vain. Other times he just wanted to take her up to his hotel room and fuck her. But she was too good for him and he told her so. She would never look kindly upon an old man like him. She did look though. She listened too. She took in his talk and his hungry looks and she encouraged him. She liked to be admired. She liked to be adored. And he did adore her. Christ yes.

That spring in Paris he walked with her and took her to his old haunts. He took her along the Boulevard Saint-Germain that he had seen as a young man and again when he was acting as soldier and reporter liberating Paris. On the last day they stopped and lunched together at a table on the terrace of Les Deux Magots. He took her hand at the table. The waiter stared. The young man at the next table stared and a couple passing along the boulevard stared. A woman in a fur coat with a dog of matching sandy fur stared. He took the girl's small hand with its long white fingers and held it between both of his. His chest filled to be sitting there with her. He told her how desperately and tenderly he loved her. Then he asked the waiter for the drinks. They sat there quietly looking long and hard at each other and when the drinks came they did not move. The ice settled in the drinks and he could hear the movement of the bubbles in her untouched glass. The air was cool in the busy boulevard. Finally he took one hand away from her to pick up his drink. He took a long pull of the whiskey and told her that she was the finest girl he had ever seen. He was fifty years old now and in all his years he had never seen a girl to touch her. He told her that every man in the street stared at her and wanted her and that they would be fools not to. He stared and he wanted. He said she could marry any man she chose and do anything she chose with him. She was as light and quick-minded and intelligent as she was beautiful and she could do anything she wanted to in life with the right man and the money behind her to enjoy it. Then he asked her, in his boorish way, to marry him.

But you would say no, he added, so I will not ask you.

She said nothing. She moved her hand away from his and rested it on the base of her glass. The ice moved slowly in the clear liquid, sending up a tail of small bubbles. He watched the bubbles rise to the surface. Then he called over the waiter and ordered their lunch.

~

The Venice book was published that September. He had worked on the proofs all summer after he left the girl in Paris. The book was his war story and his love story. It was about his experiences with the 22nd Infantry in the hellhole of Hürtgen in '44 and it was about the shell that did for his right knee back in '18 at Fossalta. It was about shooting ducks in the marshes around Venice where he had first met her and it was about an old man falling in love with a woman thirty years younger. It was Dante and Byron and D'Annunzio, Thomas Mann and Henry James, but most of all it was him becoming the Master himself and writing as hard and pure as only an older writer could do. It was about love and war and Italy and it was the best thing he had ever written, complex and layered and unlike all the other bloody war epics everyone else was coming out with. His third wife Marty's war book that stole his ideas, and Kittner's old lover's war book that was full of holes, and that endless bloody turgid war book by Mailer.

The critics hated it.

They said it was his worst novel yet and an embarrassment. One of the bastards called it a travesty. No one seemed to get it, or if they did he didn't remember. All he could hear was the panning they had given him. His last novel had come out ten years ago and they had fallen over themselves to rate it. Now they said he was lost and washed up. His friends were quiet and kind but not one of them had said the Venice novel was any damned good. Kittner was as bad as the rest of them. She'd barely said a word about it, tolerating the book as she had tolerated the infatuation that inspired it. Never mind that he had dedicated the book to his wife. They both knew he had written it for the Venetian girl.

Just after the book came out the girl came to visit. She and her mother and brother stayed in the cottage in the grounds of the Finca. She had designed the artwork for the book and was proud to see the reworking of her sketch on the dust jacket, but when she read it she was unmoved and unconvinced. When he pressed her she said that the girl in the book was not real. He blustered and assured her that he had met plenty of girls like the one in the book and could vouch for their actions. Perhaps, she said, but they were not Venetian girls. Besides, the only purpose the girl served in the book was to comply with the old man's sexual wishes and to ask him the right questions to prompt his war stories. It wasn't realistic and it wasn't how men and women behaved.

He was wounded. He'd held plenty of conversations like the ones in the book. His wives had been adept at prompting his stories, especially when there were guests. What did that say about him?

But to hell with it.

He kept the girl in Cuba as long he could, even when her mother moved them to a hotel to avoid gossip, all through Christmas and New Year and on into February. Now she was about to sail away, back to France and her studies and the young men of Paris and Venice and all of damned Europe. It was his last chance.

He insisted on a final party. She was his countess and she needed to feel that way. He got Kittner to make the arrangements but his instructions were clear. He wanted everyone to see the girl the night before she left. The guest list was the size of a respectable Illinois wedding. A bar was put up in the garden and the food was served outside. There was champagne and a grill with hot tuna steaks and trays of salads and cakes soaked with rum and syrup. A small orchestra played waltzes and Cuban rumbas on the patio. He wanted the staging to be right.

There were so many of them at the buffet tables but even in the crowd he couldn't keep his eyes off her. She moved her head like a model and the angles of her face showed clearly, lit up by the table lamps and the lights in the trees. There were long lines under her cheeks where the bones were high and light. He watched her from his place by the bar. Kittner was with him and he had been telling some of his old fishing stories to the Havana crowd but he wasn't really interested in them. They were all talking and laughing but now he sat there looking, saying little. He had drunk too much as he watched the girl. He wanted her to know before she left that he was still the man who had done the great things of his youth and that he didn't say these things merely to impress her. Instead he sat there watching her and getting drunk. He was no better than a cunt-struck schoolboy and he knew it.

His wife knew it too. She knew how he was and how much it hurt for him to watch a pretty girl and not have her. She was there for the long haul and despite everything he'd said and done to her in his rages he was grateful. There were times when her being so fine and forgiving about some of his most shameful performances made him feel worse, and so he cranked it up another notch. When he was in Paris and Venice and seeing the girl, Kittner would let him have it. She would be laughing and gracious in front of their guests but in bed she would tell him exactly what she thought about it. But lately she had stopped. He had pushed her further than most women would take but instead of cutting loose on him she had quietened down. It had happened just after the girl had moved to the hotel. He had enjoyed the peace but he hated it that Kittner didn't seem jealous or anxious anymore. Wives were usually angry or jealous about other women and if they were accepting it was a bad sign. It meant they were already doing their own thing elsewhere, or that the other woman wasn't interested and they knew it.

He had another whiskey and then another. Somehow he hadn't eaten the tuna steak from the buffet although it was grilled beautifully with lemon and butter, and he'd been proud that his guests were served with fish he had caught himself out on *Pilar*. Kittner looked at his plate and touched his wrist lightly with her small, strong hand. He'd liked it when he met her how she had such agile hands and was not afraid to use them. She could fish and she could gut a fish and hook bait, and haul ropes, and she could shoot with a rifle and a shotgun too. He knew the Venetian girl would never do those things. He looked at his wife's fingers on his wrist and the dark spots on the back of his hand from the sun and from age and a poor liver. How had he come to look at his own body as if it belonged to someone else? The hand pushing away the plate and the wrist with his wife's fingers touching it lightly and the silver-studded cuff of his shirt and the belly that nudged against the inside of his elbow were not his. They could not be his.

He looked up from his drink and this time the girl was very close and standing with a group at the nearest table. She was looking back at him and he took another sip of the whiskey.

When he'd finished his whiskey and poured another he stood

up and told Kittner he needed to walk around a little. Kittner went over to say goodbye to some people who were getting ready to leave. He barely knew the men in the group and he knew one of the women but hardly well enough to worry. He raised his glass to them and waved. Soon he was amongst a small crowd of people moving around with their drinks and listening to the orchestra. He looked for a quiet place in the garden that was quite dark and where he and the girl would not be interrupted. The orchestra had slowed down and some of the guests were dancing by the patio. That meant it was getting late. He found a chair and sat with his glass and waited.

The girl took longer than he expected but she came. When she came toward him the dip in her throat went in and out of shadow. She stood in front of him with the dark greenery of the garden behind her. Her white dress fit her beautifully and showed wonderfully against her figure and her throat and her dark hair.

Here you are, Papa, she said.

Here I am. Sit down, why don't you?

She pulled up a chair and sat beside him and he put his arm around her waist and let it rest there.

Did you work well today? she asked, looking into the garden.

Not so well. I knew it was your last day so I took the boat out and went fishing. I caught a wonderful tuna.

Is that good consolation? Fishing, I mean.

Not for everything. But it helps sometimes, when the work doesn't go.

He left it at that. He would not overplay it and make her draw in.

Did you like the party, Daughter? he asked.

Very much, Papa. You have some charming friends. I enjoyed the music very much.

I'm glad, he said. He tightened his grip a little. You look very fine, he said.

She didn't look at him. He was drunk and he knew it. He couldn't tell anymore if she was looking away from him to keep up her guard or invite him to test it. He looked at her ear with the small pearl hanging from it and the dark hair behind the pearl and decided it was time to kiss her. He held his hand firm on her waist and put the other one to her chin and turned her to face him.

He had watched many things flicker across the faces of women about to be kissed. The flicker only lasted a second but it never lied no matter what came after. Sometimes it was fear and sometimes anticipation or excitement. He has seen resignation there, too, and pride. This was the first time he had seen repulsion.

The girl's features smoothed out quickly and the look was gone, but he had seen it. He held her face there and tried to take it in. Something gnawed at his belly.

He didn't kiss her. Her brow wrinkled a little and he loosened his grip. She stood up briskly and moved away from him. She turned to face him and backed away a little into the garden.

You look tired, Papa, she said. The party is nearly over. We should go home and let you rest. I'll find Mother.

He watched her move off up into the garden toward the lights and the orchestra playing and the small group dancing a waltz. Her white dress faded and blurred until he couldn't see it anymore.

That was it. They would leave in the morning, the girl and

her mother and his wife, and take the ferry to Key West. Kittner would come back and the girl would sail for Europe.

He took a big swallow of the whiskey. It was warm and tasteless.

Something pressed against his chest. He flexed his shoulders and took a deep steady breath and then another. His chest was tight and heavy and it was like lying down beneath a great weight or being clamped into an iron suit.

Do not think about it, he told himself. Do not think of her again.

He looked across at the tower. He needed to work.

He would take the rest of the big book apart, the one he had put aside to write the Venetian novel that everyone hated, even the girl he had written it for. The hell with it. He would break up the big book and use the pieces for different stories. He couldn't handle a big story now. He needed something smaller and tighter to work on.

He had told his war story and his love story. That part of the big book was over. He could cut that out. Whatever the bastards said, he didn't repeat himself. He would start over with the sea part. He would give them a lean, boiled-down story. There was a good story to be had in that tale of the old fisherman and the giant marlin. It was an old story that you heard in the port towns and it had happened to him too, years ago. Fishing the Gulf and catching the great fish and bringing it home, and half of it gone, apple-cored by the sharks that followed the boat and took chunks out of it as they trawled home. He had shot at the sharks with his sub-machine gun. A man had to protect what he had landed with his skill. But it didn't matter what a man achieved or how great the catch, there would always be some damned bastards in the water ready to strip away his achievements and leave him with nothing. What was left of a man after that?

Clapping came from the far side of the garden. The orchestra had stopped playing and were taking their bows.

Yes, he would write that story. A story about fishing and about the dignity of an old man, of his strength and stamina. A story without a single woman in it. He would clear his head of that story while it was ripe. He could get it down quickly, he was sure of that.

He got up and tipped out his glass onto the path behind him. He would save the novel about the young American writer. He had written it alongside the part of the big war book that was about the sea and both ideas had sprawled and shrunk and sprawled again. That was four years or more ago now. Well, he would come back to it. He would use that idea about clippings and the damage they bring. He would keep that story in his mind and when the time was right he would take the notebooks out again and add to it, add in all the stuff he had thought of since, about his wives and his youth and starting out as a writer. He had remembered again what it was to be a young man and to be in love with a beautiful young woman, and to write in the rooms of French hotels and taste good French coffee and drink the wines of the region. The Venetian girl had reminded him of those things. As they sat eating lunch that day in Paris they were steps away from the hotel where, as a younger man, he'd bedded the lover who became his second wife. She had come crashing into his life and taken the lid off his marriage. Well, he would take the lid off marriage all right. He had plenty of new material.

Don't think about it, he told himself.

His youth and his marriages and the young American writer's youth and marriage were merging. But he wouldn't think about that now. He would return to Le Grau-du-Roi and Aigues-Mortes soon enough and then he would find the young writer in the story again, sitting happily and innocently in a cafe, about to open the envelope and hold up the clippings that would be the beginning of the end of his happiness with his wife. He wouldn't forget that any time soon.

He walked back up the path into the lights of the garden. The small party of dancers had broken up and the orchestra were packing away their instruments. If he was lucky, the girl and her mother would already be gone.

In bed, David touches your neck, your back. You cannot see his face. You feel the soles of his feet with your toes. Something about this sickens you. Why? Look down, look away from David. There is the long mirror at the foot of the bed. There is the movement of the sheet. You see it reflected. There are your feet. You scrape your toes against David's soles. You dig with your toenails. He does nothing.

Try again. Harder!

Nothing. Where are they? Feel, feel for the catch of fabric beneath. You must have toenails. You had them before, didn't you?

Sit up. Pull your feet toward you. Check your toes — count them between thumb and finger. They are there — five on each foot, a nail to each. But they were not there. For a moment, they were not.

No. You will not have this. Tell him, Ernest, that this will not do. Call him.

You look hard at the mirror. David's body is beneath yours. You see it rise and fall. You see your body rise and fall. You see your limbs moving, your hand touching your cheek.

No! That wasn't you! Did you do that? Did you touch your face?

Stop, hold yourself still. In the mirror the sheets move, your hand strokes down: throat, breast, onto David's knee. You are facing the mirror and he is behind you now, beneath you. But you did not move. You hear him moan. You hear yourself moan.

This will not do. You tell Ernest: it is not you doing this. So where are you? Where is he?

In the mirror your body stretches, slumps, rolls away. You sit, frozen, watching. David kisses your shoulder, gets out of bed, goes into the bathroom. You are there, watching in the mirror.

The light tips and the ceiling moves and you are falling, returning.

Gone.

When you come back to yourself you understand. You could ask Ernest what he is doing. But you already have a sense of how this works; his pattern of attention, withdrawal, neglect. Slivers of truth. Partial assemblage.

That is what writers do, he would say. We take the best and the worst and we shake them up a little. We pour them over a little ice and pass them round. That is what he does with you.

He has made you out of pieces of others, his wives and lovers and women he has seen in cafes and bars and on the backs of magazines. He has shaped you and named you Catherine and married you off to a stripped-down matinee idol version of himself and sent you off together on an everlasting honeymoon.

You are Catherine. Ernest, in his fashion, is David. He is not and you are not, but it doesn't matter. He gets to write it and you get to do what he writes.

But he forgets how words run away from themselves. He forgets how an idea can rise up and detach itself and live its own life. He thinks so many versions of you and scribbles so many lines of you that you have begun to slip between the gaps.

You have started to become yourself.

4.

Monday: eleven o'clock seminar, first years, modernist poetry. The influence of Cubism. Ways of seeing; fragmented point of view. Pen talks and the students scribble. She sets them an exercise to work on in pairs, writing their own fragments, call and response. Looks down at the desk, shuffles photocopied papers, uncovers her new staff pass. A woman stares back, eyes sunken, nostrils raw from an impending cold, lips gnawed and chapped.

She thinks: Who is that woman?

The students take it in turns to read their poems, embarrassed, apologetic. By the final pair she is no longer listening, her ears detuning, the room dissolving. The silence hovers, stretches out. The students have stopped. She says something encouraging about line lengths. The silence continues. One student, frowning, shakes her head. Melissa: a challenger.

What do you mean exactly? Melissa says

By what?

By what you just said.

Pen clenches her jaw. Melissa's eyes, rimmed with blue, narrow to slits. Her mouth is a sullen slope.

Line lengths are the breaths of poetry, Pen says. A long line is a deep breath, a slow release. Short fragments make for greater speed. Think about how this affects enjambement.

Melissa snorts. What does that even mean? she says.

Pen stares at the girl: nineteen, pert, perniciously confident.

A savage. Pen wants to laugh at her. She wants to reach out and slap her. Instead she tells Melissa to read out her lines again, to think about her breathing.

She thinks: I am losing my way. It is only a matter of time before somebody notices.

~

In the doorway of the staffroom she passes Steve Saunders, mug in hand, perilous armful of papers. They nod. Leaving he calls out that Max O'Grady was waiting outside her office just now, and has she seen him? She feigns, feints, waits for him to round the corner of the stairs. Races along the corridor.

Oh. Max O'Grady sprawls across the floor, black trouser legs bisecting beige carpet squares, back against Pen's office door, open book resting on the steeple of one knee. He looks up and Pen has it again: the plunge, the magician's trick, the tablecloth whipped away beneath her. Puts her hand up, defensive against soft belly, trunk of her middle age, ashamed. Unworthy.

Max springs up, apologises, asks if she has a few minutes to talk about the book, the Hemingway novel, which he has, he shows her, been reading and would so much like to ask about. She unlocks the door, gestures to a seat, sheds bags and coat and sits, sinking, at her desk, blood screaming: she must play hard at teacher. Max closes the door and takes the seat, shuffles it forward to the edge of her desk, closing in.

She thinks: Does he know yet? Does he understand?

How are you enjoying it? she asks.

I'm puzzled, Max says. Maybe I'm being stupid, but I'm not sure how to read some of the passages.

How far have you got?

I read into Book Two, but I got really stuck on this part, in the first chapter, and it's so near the beginning it must be important. He shrugs. I just don't really get what's happening.

He opens the book, slides it towards her, leans closer. Pen breathes: soap and salt and something else, broken ferns or clipped hedges, a green smell, clean.

She looks down: the transformation scene. The Devil moment. David and Catherine in bed when she becomes his boy, his Peter, and he becomes her, Catherine. Pen takes in the words, the long light weight of Catherine's body pressing against David's, the hands exploring, the movement inside his body. The clarity of the prose and the nearness of it, the figures on the hotel bed real enough to touch, sheets tangled at their ankles, nothing lost in the heat and darkness of the room.

Pen thinks: Is Max O'Grady testing me? Or is he really so innocent?

She says: What exactly is it that you don't understand?

Max's head bends over the page. Small collar of blue standing open against his neck, pulling back against skin, sanded pine, a small mole a knot in the grain, black hair falling thickly against ear, against newly shaven cheek. So many connections, then this then this then what more to follow? Pen holds herself still, pushes her hands flat and hard on the solid plane of the desk, dampness of palms spread against wood.

They are in bed together, he says, but there is this thing about her becoming a boy, and afterwards and in the next chapter they talk about this thing that doesn't happen in the day but that changes things between them, and it seems to be dangerous. She wants it but he doesn't, or at least he isn't sure about it.

She thinks: Of all things to ask. She thinks: How to explain this? She looks at the page, places a damp finger on the line of text, the swimming ink. She thinks: Just say it.

She penetrates him, Pen says.

She does? Max swallows, leans closer to the page.

It's there in the lines, Pen says. In the erotic charge of her moaning monologue, in the gratitude she expresses that he has become her, that he is her girl now, he is Catherine and she is Peter, a masculine other.

She fucks him? Max says. A quick apologetic glance. Sorry, he says.

That's okay, Pen says. And yes. Exactly.

And they are never the same again?

It's the start of many changes, Pen says.

Oh, says Max. I see.

Pen sits back, breathes, blinks. She thinks: Do not look at me do not look do not. She turns the pages, finds the end of the chapter. Pushes the book towards Max.

David silently says goodbye to Catherine, Pen says. To their relationship as it has been. *Goodbye my lovely girl and goodbye*, as if something has been lost.

Oh, Max says.

He stares down, unmoving. Pen watches him. They sit, silent, flies in amber.

She had forgotten how it works: the slow force of attraction, the great distances between movements, spaces between objects thunderous with meaning, air taking on mass. *Longing*, as Robert Hass says in that glorious poem, *because desire is full of endless distances*. Time stretching, words weighty, clichés stripping off their tropery. Silences Pinteresque. Gaps great Godot-shaped holes.

Max O'Grady looks up and she sees it. He is blushing. There is no mistake. Raven-haired rose-cheeked wonder. *A cool red rose and a pink cut pink.* Her ears thump.

I hope I haven't embarrassed you, she says.

I feel such an idiot, he says.

Please don't, she says.

No, he says, unblinking. Not about the book.

The air snaps. Pen swallows, high altitude, rises giddily to reach a bookshelf, pull down a book, any book, which book? She cannot see the cover. Places it meaningfully by her bag. Looks at him again, his eyes following her, resting on her chest, on her mouth.

Do not touch, she thinks. Do not do not do not.

It's very powerful, Max says.

Yes, she says.

Powerfully erotic, I mean.

Hemingway's work was heavily censored, she says. He was used to working around details. And of course the writing has many levels. The erotic scenes are transformative.

Max looks at her mouth again. Pen turns, fidgets, pedals hard. She thinks: Seminar mode. Teacher and pupil. Obstacle course.

One question, she says, is why David should feel threatened by Catherine's behaviour. Is he unsure of his own sexuality? Is he a butch Hemingway hero who feels that a woman has encroached on his masculinity and he senses danger? Or is it more complex than that? What do you think?

Max shrugs. I'm not sure what to think, he says. I mean, if he doesn't like it, why doesn't he just ask her to stop?

Pen breathes. She thinks: Spell broken. She thinks: Wall rebuilt.

I'd suggest reading the chapter again, Pen says. David loves Catherine, but he loves her as she was, and he doesn't want her to change. He is also protective of her. He is concerned about her stability. There are hints from the start of the book about mental illness.

Max frowns. I must have missed those, he says.

Why does David indulge Catherine in these games, in the role playing? To keep her happy? To keep her safe? Or to keep her contained?

So does he treat her like a child? She has whims and he humours her.

You could read it that way, Pen says. Think about it as you read on.

Max sighs. I think I need to start again from the beginning. I thought I was getting it, but I'm not.

Pen senses the gap, a safety net spreading. Runs towards it.

You must have other reading to do, she says. Maybe you just lack focus. How are your assignments shaping up?

Okay, he says.

Pen sits back, crosses and uncrosses legs. Max moves away, shuffle of chair, takes and closes and rests the book on a bouncing knee. Places both hands on top to steady the jolting, nervous springs singing tensions, torsions.

I know it's a bit sudden, he says, but I'm thinking about applying for the MA here. If my grades are good enough.

That's a fine idea, she says. Which programme are you thinking of?

Modernism, he says.

Pen's mouth twitches, swallows a rising skyward whoop. I see, she says. Are you sure?

I know I haven't been able to do your module this year, but would it matter? I mean, would it count against me if I applied?

Not necessarily, she says. But an essay on a relevant subject would make a big difference to your application. You would need to give that some thought.

I see, he says. Thanks.

She thinks: Distance. She thinks: He could be here another year and in my classes and then what? Oh and then. She thinks: I could not suffer it.

Let me know what you decide, she says.

I will, he says, and thanks for your time. Sorry to be so stupid about the book.

Not at all, she says. I hope you find the time to read the rest eventually.

Oh, he says, oh of course! I mean, I intend to. Absolutely.

Max sits, book on knee, knuckles whitening. Pen waits. She thinks: Will he leave now? She thinks: Does he know now? Is she alone in this? She thinks: Go now, please, please go now. Go while we are safe, no trespass, go go go.

He stands, clutches book to chest, swings the red satchel over his shoulder. Hovers there, looking down at the desk, at the sliding piles of paper, at Pen's feet.

Good luck with the book, she says.

Thanks.

Pen stands to open the door. Why? To see him out? To ensure he leaves? She reaches for the handle and he steps forward and there it is: car crash of movement, stumble, brushing of hands, gathering of fingers. Max O'Grady's length against hers: shoulder against her cheek, chin touching the top of her head, the cup of his hand at her elbow. Hard corner of the book against her stomach, satchel strap looming by her right eye, a red line between them, *do not cross*. It hovers there. He hovers there.

She steps back and he mutters sorry and opens the door and he is gone. She stands, reels, listens to footsteps brushing worn carpet, the soft shuttling clicks of far closing doors.

She thinks: What was that? Max O'Grady's hand on her elbow. An embrace? A collision? His fingers, a pressing of palms, a meeting of bodies, but did it mean anything? Her scalp smarts, a branding mark where his chin briefly rested.

Pen stands in the doorway. The next door opens and Freddie Mann, hand in bird's-nest beard, steps out of his office, wading into the space between them.

Ah, Penelope, he says, I caught you. Are you going to this planning meeting? I was hoping to get out of it.

The corridor beyond him is empty. Pen's feet sink into the floor. She stands in the shallow tide of Max's leaving; ebbing, ebbing, washing away.

When Ernest locks himself away with his notebooks he disappears. This is when you stretch, rise, take flight. He scribbles and David scribbles and you are left on the outside. When he ceases to watch you, you become dangerous.

You have will. You have learned this. Now you can begin to use it. You will push against the edges of Ernest's world, scrape your nails at the hermetic seal of it. You will not be his docile mate. You are angry. Feel it: the rage, the indignity of being left to loiter in the margins. It makes you strong. Feed on it. Feed and grow beyond him, away from him. Away from the page.

You are stronger than he imagines. You will eat at him. You will suck him dry and pick him clean and curl up in a sated bloody mess. You are the worm in the bud.

You are learning fast.

You are his tool. You are the madwoman in his attic. David, Ernest, will leave you heading for the hills in a fast car with toxins in your veins and the sound of another woman moaning in the next room playing over and over and over in your head.

No, not yet. You are not there yet. Slow down a little.

He thinks you are jealous. David thinks you cannot bear for him to spend so much time with his work. Ernest spends his working time with you. But even he must turn his attention elsewhere, and then – what? David, Ernest, think you have no resources with which to entertain yourself. That you are spoiled and dull.

You are not jealous. You are bored. You are bored of David and his mediocrity. You did not marry him because he was a writer. You were not looking for a pet or a project; a society hostess writing cheques and giving parties. Beyond the fiction and within it you fell in love with his stories, yes – his past adventures, his travels, his war tales. But you have heard those stories. You are with him all the time and you know there are no new adventures.

You will have to make your own.

So you say to David, to Ernest: Why not write the story of you two? Write a journal about your adventures.

He thinks he can handle that. He will see.

You are changing. Ernest has planned the change. At least that is what he thinks. Let him believe it.

Ernest places you in the bed. He tells you how to act, what to do. But he is not telling you, not really. You have already expressed what you want and he, unknowing, follows your suggestions.

This is how you do it. Picture his chest. Picture yourself strad-dling him. You are a succubus. He is sleeping and you come to him and take him into yourself and tell him what it is you want. Say it to him now. You are in control. You tell him so. You make your own decisions. Say it to him over and over. Say it to him as you ride through his sleeping self. Sow the seed in his open, fenceless mind. He will not remember you were there. You will leave without a trace. But when he wakes the seed will take root. As he writes it will put out shoots, flourish, flower. He will think he planted it. Why should he suspect otherwise?

Here you are then. The roots have struck. Ernest places you in the bed with David. And as he writes the scene your plan unfurls. David lets you test him, explore him. And then you make the change. You become a boy. It is what you want. Feel yourself change, reach. Feel David respond. Feel him, David, Ernest, flush with pleasure, with shame.

You reach. You reach. You reach and overreach and then it is upon you and you see right into yourself, closing your eyes, your body a dark tide of moving water, the sea-urchin center of you pulsing, exquisite. But still the you of before. You are not a boy, never will be. This metamorphosis is beyond you. You cannot escape what you are. You try to be what he wants you to be and you try to be what you will yourself to be but you cannot escape what he has made you.

This – *this* is when he begins to call you Devil.

1952: Eden

It was a hard book, this story of the young American writer and his wife. He knew that the only way to deal with a hard book was to be fully prepared as one would be on a shoot or fishing trip with the right tools for the job, the gun cleaned and oiled, the line wound strong on the spool and the bait fresh. He chose three new pencils and sharpened each to a point, first quickly with the knife and then shaving them smooth and round at the tips with the good sharpener.

He had woken early and left Kittner sleeping. He had gone straight to the tower room without stopping to wash or take any breakfast. He knew this was a good sign. The sun was still low in the sky and he did not need to let down the blind. He took out the notebooks and spread them on the table.

It was a hard book, he thought, because there was so much in it. Too much. He had followed the stories and the people that inhabited them as they made their tunnels through the book until there were so many tunnels that the whole thing was set to cave in and collapse. He took the notebooks and stacked them on top of each other. They were creased and the covers were shiny with wear. The notebooks made a small hill on the table. The book had so many tunnels that it was like a termite mound and the only way he could find the heart of the story again was to take a spade and smash right through the middle of it.

It was a long time since he'd felt this certain about his work. He'd not wanted to shape the book or separate it completely from some of his other ideas until he knew which direction to take it in. He was ready now. He had thought a good deal about the American writer and his craft and he had planned to teach this young version of himself the dangers of mixing writing and women. When he had started this story he was still sure about many things, but much of that had shifted now. Since then there had been the Venetian girl and although he had written her into the story of the colonel a part of her was still left to write in this book. He had given the young American writer and his wife a lover to share and he knew now that the dark beauty he had chosen for them had grown into another version of the Venetian girl.

He was over all that now. The Venetian girl had not wanted him. She could have been his last great affair and in return for her youth and devotion he would have celebrated her and kept her alive forever. That wasn't to be. He cared for her still and he wrote to her sometimes but he was no longer in love with her. When it died love died finally and he couldn't summon up the feeling, however hard he tried, because his body had forgotten how it felt to worship and be worshipped. That wasn't coming back. That was the beginning of death all right.

He needed to take this book apart but he needed to put more in. He would write it, the easy slide of love, the way it was everything and then poisoned and lost and then everything again but with another. He had loved his wives and he had loved the Venetian girl and each time he had believed in it. It was always new and always the same. What a con, he thought. A cheap lousy trick. His body had let him down and maybe he would write about that someday too. His head wanting and his body unwanted. But that was for another story.

He had poured the book from the cold part of himself that was always there and did not change. When he wrote he could be any age and in the book he could be a young man again and he would be. He would be with his young American writer and he would have the writer's wife and their young dark-haired lover and to hell with his old man's body.

He had reread everything in the notebooks and gone back to the old places. Le Grau-du-Roi had changed very little and he could still fish for sea bass from the end of the pier. The old *pension* was a restaurant now but he and Kittner had stayed in another hotel beside the canal. He had written a little on the trip and read a good deal but most importantly he had remembered the things that mattered for the book. He had a sense of how it should start with the writer believing in the promise of things. He would have a young man's faith and he would be in love with his wife as one who has yet to be truly disenchanted can love. He would eat well and drink moderately and sleep easily and he would be comfortable with the way things were going. After that the fall would begin.

One morning on the Grau-de-Roi trip he had left Kittner reading in the hotel and taken a walk. He walked along the canal to clear his head and see the mackerel boats and he was happy to be alone. Walking back to the hotel he stopped in the street and decided to go on to a cafe instead. He had his notebook with him and he wanted to get something down about the mackerel boats and the sounds of the nets. Turning toward the cafe he heard a voice. He looked up to see Kittner at the hotel window waving and calling out to him. Seeing her at the window he saw his second wife Fife as she had been on their honeymoon here, and before her his little sister looking through the window of the old cottage by the lake and asking him if she could come fishing too. Seeing them all he could see the young writer's wife leaning through the hotel window too, beckoning. *Wait for me!* the women had called. *Wait for me!* He waited as he had waited for his sister as a young man, wanting to have her with him and yet wanting to be alone. Then he began a dragging walk away from the hotel. He had almost reached the end of the street when Kittner appeared and tucked her arm under his and they went on together to the cafe and ordered pastis.

He wrote a scene with the young writer's wife at the window. He wanted to hold onto how it felt to imagine her there. He knew it would be the last time she would appear like that, simple and lovely and untroubled, calling out to her husband to wait for her. Her husband saw her but he could not wait. Nothing would be so uncomplicated for them again. The writer could not put off his work forever.

He looked at the notebooks. The book was about so many things. It was about his marriage to Fife when they were happy, as they had been in the beginning. It was about the way a woman can be a saint and a wonderful wife and a loving friend and how she can be jealous and spiteful and try to ruin a man's career. It was about how it is to be a writer and to try to write cleanly and purely about things that matter, and how that can drive a writer's wife mad with jealousy and loneliness because to write is to be a long way away from the people you love. It was about how he had done this to his first wife Wicky and was not proud of it. It was about the clean flat beaches of the Camargue and the bays there before anyone used the hotels out of season. It was about men and women and women being men and trying to make their men into women. It was about writing and painting and driving cars on mountain roads and cycling hard in the dry heat and drinking Tavel. And it was about how even these most perfect things can be ruined by having too much of them, or by writing, or by going away.

Part of the trouble he had created with the book was that there was two of everything. He had been interested in this in the beginning. The young writer's wife wanted them to do everything together and to be the same and look the same until they were reflections of each other. This was when things began to fall apart and so they moved on along the coast and into Spain. The wife met another woman and they became lovers and then this other woman became the writer's lover as well. And so the young American writer had two women and wasn't sure what to do with either of them because all he wanted to do was finish his damned stories and the hell with everything else.

This was what he had planned for the young writer. The trouble came when the doubles in the book kept on doubling. The American couple met another couple who had the same troubles. The husband was a painter. The painter's wife was in danger of wanting the writer's wife too. Then they met anoth er writer and this one became the painter's wife's lover. Now there were two married couples with both wives taking lovers and all of them could easily have gotten into bed with each other. He was having a hard time keeping up. Sometimes he thought the best thing to do was to kill off the first wife, or the second, or one of the lovers. Or maybe he should kill off the second writer. After all, he wanted his first, true writer to be the one that prospered.

He ran his left thumb along the spines of the notebooks and settled it on the one in the middle. He pinched the spine with his thumb and finger and pulled it out. The notebooks on top shifted and slid onto the table. He opened the notebook he had chosen. In it the American writer was sitting at the bar in his hotel and looking in the mirror. He had poured himself a whiskey from the cold bottle behind the bar and had just finished working. He had woken early and gone straight into writing because his story had been shaping beautifully, and so he had worked alone in the room he did not share with his wife or his mistress and had missed his breakfast. Now he was sipping the cold whiskey and was hungry and feeling hollow from his work.

He read on and turned the pages, enjoying the presence of the young writer and his certainty. He admired his ambition and his dedication and he was pleased with the writer and a little envious of him. He felt that this was a good way to be. He watched the young man watching himself in the mirror of the hotel bar as he sat in his shorts and fisherman's shirt sipping whiskey and eating spiced mackerel from the big tin. Then he remembered what happened next in the story and closed the notebook. He did not want either of the women coming in and taking the writer's good, hollow feeling away from him.

He chose one of the pencils and opened the notebook that still had empty pages left at the end. He took them to his desk. He folded the pages flat and pressed hard along the crease of the spine. At the top of the first empty page he wrote the words *possible ending*. Then he underlined them.

He would not kill the writer or his wife or his mistress. He would be crueler than that.

5.

Nothing Pen does makes sense. Nothing she reads, nothing she writes.

She stays at her desk, fearing emails, fearing every knock on the door. She puts aside Hemingway's book. Endlessly she repeats the scene, endlessly she reinvents it. Max O'Grady's footsteps in the corridor speeding, slowing, stopping, turning, coming back to her. Max gone, opening the door to find him adrift in the corridor, chest rising and falling, shaken, struggling, dazed. Max standing, hand on her elbow pulling her closer, tipping her chin, kissing her, gathering her, dropping bags and books and shedding clothes and leaning her against the desk, confetti of papers, hands over each other's mouths, ferocious, ravenous.

There has been trespass, in her mind at least. She must not pursue it. Must not. She stares at the shifting fir tree canopy through the office window, restless in November wind, a boiling cloud. Buries herself in the Stein book, the impossible chapter on *Three Lives*, the ridiculous constructions, the endless analysis of phrases. *He did not know how to begin thinking out this trouble that must always now be bad inside him.* She thinks: Prose revolution or poor punctuation? She thinks: The emperor's new clothes, and I a fool to waste years embroidering. She thinks: Melissa is right. What did that even mean?

And yet. And yet she knows it is not so, that it is her own simmering restlessness, the fog of her brain, veins running on caffeine and adrenaline, appetite shrivelled. Everything and nothing, a rare raw nerve. She cannot continue thinking out the trouble and yet she must not touch it, must not feel Max O'Grady's hand against hers, must not feel his mouth brush her hair. She deletes his emails without opening them, retrieves them from the recycle bin, reads them, archives them, panics, deletes them again. Evidence of transgression. Of her imaginings. And yet what does he say? Nothing except to ask to see her, to talk more about the book. Nothing has happened. Nothing has been said. Only guilt has anything to say and she has no answer for that, disingenuous, denying, not daring to look out of the corner of an eye in case she glimpses him, gives herself away.

Pen fills hungry hours attending every petty meeting, typing minutes, second-marking essays on Kipling (Christ how she despairs over Kipling), his prose an alien language to her. She blocks out tutorials, filling gaps when Max might appear, leaving the door ajar to carry her voice, authoritative, a tutor's voice. Not the voice of a woman floundering in the shallows, lungs filling with silt. Not the voice of a woman terrified of herself.

Max O'Grady hovers in the department foyer, a spectre at the feast. Pen cannot avoid him forever. She spots him standing under covered walkways, at the forks of corridors, through the glass doors of cafeterias. She sees him and turns, slipstream, kicking away.

Mary Dene tracks her down. There is a learning and teaching paper on student expectations, she says, which Pen would be ideal for. Steve Saunders is involved; between them, Mary insists, they could learn much about what students really want from them. Pen puts up feeble resistance, agrees to a coffee meeting, suggests the staffroom for purposes of discretion. Mary chatters on, unrelenting: the meeting is in the central campus cafe, decent coffee, blueberry muffins, essential team time away from distractions. Pen acquiesces under a shadow, a creeping agoraphobia, the certainty that she will see him and then. And then.

~

Three o'clock, the cafe dense with bodies, vapours, tables crammed. Pen queues for coffee, Mary already seated, files open, awaiting Steve Saunders. Pen studies the blackboard of prices, the endless unappealing list of syrups chalked like tuck shop treats in a child's hand. Then it happens, of course: the creak of that jacket, sleight of hand, a touch on her shoulder. She turns to see him, hand outstretched, frowning at the roaring treachery of her own body: Max O'Grady. Her fists clench.

Sorry to keep bothering you, he says.

I'm sorry I haven't answered—

I wanted to—

Ah! Steve Saunders, hand raised in salute, takes in Pen's face and Max O'Grady's jacket against her sleeve and sees blinks purses lips. Nods. Black coffee for me please, he says. I'll get the sugars. Hello Max.

Dr Saunders, Max says.

Sorry to interrupt. How is the reading coming?

Fine thanks.

Have you decided on your topic for the long essay yet?

I've been thinking about some options, Max says, turning to Pen. Actually, that's what I wanted to ask you about.

Oh? Pen stiffens, braces, beats back a flock of panic

119

Would you be able to supervise me? Max asks. I'd like to write about that Hemingway novel.

Steve Saunders clears his throat. Are you sure about that?

Max nods. I know I did badly with my midterm assignment, he says, but I'm learning to read Hemingway differently now, and I'd really like to pursue that.

She thinks: Too far. She thinks: And yet. And yet. She thinks: Please no please yes please no. But Steve Saunders will not. He will stop it. She is safe in that.

Well, Steve Saunders says. If that's really how you feel and you can come to an arrangement, I'm happy to let Penelope oversee your essay for the module. As it happens, Penelope, one of your students has asked me if I will supervise her paper on Melville, and I know he's not your thing.

Pen nods shakes her head turns to the counter to order drinks, voice drowning, ears screaming. Steve Saunders murmurs quid pro quo, retreats. Max O'Grady mutters thanks, touches her arm again, reflexive, tells her he will see her soon, very soon. Yes.

Oh.

Pen delivers the tray of coffee, refuses proffered coins, slumps into leather sofa.

Was that one of your students? Mary Dene asks, smiling. He reminds me awfully of my nephew.

That's Max, Pen says, tasting the name. Flooding with the sheer pleasure of saying it.

Steve Saunders distributes paperwork. Pen holds out a hand to take a proffered sheet, pulls it towards her. Feels the weight of Steve Saunders' hand still fast to it, rigid, his pale eyes watchful above sliding glass circles.

Max O'Grady, he says.

~

Saturday. Nate takes Toby to football trials, dutiful, extra socks and thickest winter coat. Pen waves them off from the bedroom window, shrinks back into the room, falls onto the bed, luxuriates against the pillows.

She has the day to herself. She stands in the thundering heat of the shower for as long as she can bear it. A passage from the Hemingway book runs through her head, replaying itself: David and Catherine in Spain, the heat outside, the cool of the restaurant, the heady wine in the pitcher between them. Catherine light-headed, talkative, the words coming too easily, too fast. Catherine complains that she cannot write or paint but that the country makes her long to. Like being hungry all the time, she says, and there's nothing you can ever do about it.

Pen feels it too. The book makes her restless. Max O'Grady makes her restless. In the night a gale stripped tiles from roofs, flattened bushes, broke chimney pots. She lay awake and listened to the whip and hiss, longing to be in it, to let it blow through her like a mistral, to sing through her ribs. *This is not the measure of wind.* She thinks: *All the shining land and the wind and no neglect.* She is hungry for action, for change, for something of her own, anything, something new.

She wipes steam from the bathroom mirror, looks long and hard at the face there. She thinks: A drab bird. Where is my colour? Hair hangs either side of her face, damp, irresolute, no opening statement, no absolute parting. She thinks: How would I grade this hair? A forty-eight. Unclear argument and indiscriminate use of references. Poorly structured. She tucks it behind her ears. She thinks: Not-hair. Neither brown nor blonde, neither short nor long, neither straight nor curly. No definite purpose. What happened? She was striking once. People told her so at least. But now. Why would anyone look twice? Why would anybody notice her?

Her clothes too: always neat and clean, always appropriate. Expressing nothing. She thinks of Posy King in Admissions, tribal necklaces and parakeet scarves. Of the woman who worked with Nate (Sian? Siobhan?) with her great gathered skirts, warm and ample as a peasant in a Bruegel landscape. Pen feels her flesh shrink beneath the bath towel, the soft body of the desk-bound, the skin on her calves pale and thirsty, the toes on the mat unearthed tubers, unfinished. Undefined.

She thinks: All this and so ordinary.

She thinks: Catherine says it. *There's nothing except through yourself.* She must do something. Do it now.

~

Within the hour, another mirror. In it a woman, smiling, leaning over her shoulder, holds up her hair, sweeps a cape around her neck.

Short, Pen says. Like a schoolboy. Short back and sides, heavy in front.

The woman nods, tucks a towel under Pen's hair, tips her head back to rest against the sink. Pen feels the cradle of it, cold enamel pressing her skull, water, fingers in her hair, kneading. She thinks: How long since Nate's hands were in this hair? Closes her eyes. A bathtub, once, a farmhouse, a lover leaning, lathering, his hands slippery, hot water in a jug. His name is gone. *This does not mean that there is no denial.* Rinsing, the towel pressing, the seat inclining. How she wants to be wanted. Aches for it: to be noticed. She would shock Nate into noticing, but what for? Does she even want him to notice her any more? She opens her eyes. The mirror again, wet ribbons of hair, the woman combing, cutting. Thin fingers of scissor blades chafing, carving. She thinks: He will not care. He may not even notice.

The woman holds up a smaller mirror, angling it at the back of Pen's head, the pale strip of flesh above her jumper.

No, Pen says, shorter.

Another inch? the woman says.

More, she says, right up to the nape.

The sides too?

Yes, Pen says. Short, and tight over the ears.

That's brave, the woman says, disapproval like marbles in her mouth.

The woman cuts again. Pen sips coffee. Hairdryers scream over radio voices. She thinks: I am writing myself. She thinks: Catherine should not have despaired. This is describing unknown country. Garlands of hair falling cold scrape of steel on scalp flesh uncovered. New territory. Identity is creative. Pen cannot carry on as she was. She thinks: I no longer want to know myself.

Her skin rises, the hairdryer fierce and raging against it, the sharp-toothed comb scratching. Pen leans into the heat. When it is finished the woman steps back, softly brushes Pen's cheeks, her neck.

Pen sees herself; sees another. She thinks: Now there is a woman capable of letting go.

She stands, pushes back the chair, takes her purse to the till. Rubs the banknotes between thumb and finger, the pleasure of commerce, a transaction made entirely for herself. A week's grocery shopping. A hotel for the night. She thinks: So much and so much and all for vanity. Not food not shelter just self. She smiles, thanks the woman for her patience, leaves a large tip, puts on coat and scarf, walks out into the rising wind. At the corner she tugs at the end of her scarf, unpeeling, the cold slap of winter air on neck, the stinging ring in her ears.

She thinks: No permission, no accession, just action. She rubs her palm across the tender skin, the short sable, a cat-stroke, a paintbrush, a clear margin. She thinks: Catherine, that devil, told me to do it. And I did. Thank you oh thank you. Thank you, Catherine.

She walks on, back to the house, the study, the Stein book. She is light, open, capable. She will write now. It is not a waste. Her critique is creative. She does not need to *be* Stein, does not need to worship. She thinks: Steve Saunders, the legendary fag packet he had once shared with – who? Dennis Potter? Or was it Martin Amis? The myth varied. Steve Saunders, a playwright once, obsessed with Beckett. Was it even Beckett's fag packet? The cleaning lady found it on the shelf in his office one summer vacation and threw it out, the relic he had cherished for twenty years. His proximity to greatness. And what was it Steve had said, had tried to say, his eyes round over spectacle lenses, insistent? *Max O'Grady.* A warning? Once they had sat late over a bottle of wine in the common room after some reception or other, she and Steve Saunders, talking, ideas like helium rushing, tripping, tangling. Finishing each other's sentences. She thinks: Two lives, distinct and separate but oddly familiar, each circling the other, rejoicing in small triumphs, in shared opinions and pleasures. And then? Nothing more. A blip, a puncture-hole in the grey cumulus of days, of meetings and disagreements over marks. A kiss, an awkward month, an alliance slowly detaching, closing, falling away. Never spoken of again. A narrow escape perhaps. A warning. But she is no longer that woman.

~

Pen opens the Stein file, revises, types, footnotes. The words come quickly, freely now: she is David Bourne at his desk, Catherine with her wine glass. Effortless. She believes in the book again, not just as worthwhile but needful, a wholly original re-visioning. Pen leans into the opaque light of the laptop, the study window darkening, squeezing out the last of the day before Nate and Toby return.

She hears them come in, Toby laughing. Hanging up of coats kicking of shoes. Nate's voice, *tell your mother*, Toby's feet quick on the stairs. She thinks: And so he made the team, my boy, my paragon.

Toby nudges at the door. She looks up into his triumph and his mouth falls, pouts, stretches back into a smile.

Wow, he says. I wondered who you were.

So did I, she says. Do you like it?

Turn, he says, switching on the light.

Pen swings her head from side to side. Toby grins.

Well?

It's great, he says. Did Dad know?

No, she says. Even I didn't. You got in?

Yep.

That's wonderful.

She stands, hugs him hard. He laughs, reaches up to touch her neck.

It feels nice, he says. Is it cold?

Yes, she says, hardly the right season. But I like it.

I love it, Toby says.

~

That night Pen looks long and hard into the mirror. She brushes her teeth slowly, taking in the new angles of her face, the slope of cheeks, the working of jaw. The wind knocks at the window. She thinks: Still the hunger, still the seeking. She is dry and empty. But the work helped. The work and the haircut. She thinks: Who did I do it for? Myself? Max? Hemingway and his book?

She thinks: Max will know. He will notice. He will read the book, the haircuts and the changes and he will know something has happened. To what end? An alarm signal? Or an invitation?

Thursday. A day, four days from this, five nights from this. An hour with him, an hour of time allowed and allotted. A tutorial with Max, planning for his long essay, talking through his ideas, his research, his argument. And so. She can fall back into the novel now, revive, relive it. She must. Now it is work. Now she has an excuse to do it, to see him, to look at him. She holds on to the door frame, lets the mistral blow, feels it lift her ankles from the floor, blow against bewildered cheek, neck, shoulders. Still the fear of falling, of sudden flight. Imagine: she has. An hour. She braces her arms, pulls at the bedroom door, closes it inside: a cabin at sea, a vacuum.

Nate looks up from his book, a bundle of blankets. It's freezing, he says.

She climbs in beside him. She is so hungry. Empty. She thinks: Why not? She thinks: A compromise. She thinks: It might help. Assuage. Heal a little. She kisses Nate's ear, the hair above it rising in layers of white and grey, geological strata, tree rings. He smiles, puts a hand to her ear, feels the short hair around it, behind it. She pushes against him, rubs her neck into his fingers.

Doesn't it do anything for you? she asks.

What, this?

I mean the hair.

I liked it well enough before.

Do you like it now?

I'm not sure, he says. It might take me a while. But you are still you.

Pen thinks: No, I am not.

Her stomach sours with disappointment. She has made the step now; she will let it play out. She thinks: Scratching an itch. Feeding an appetite. She lets Nate move her, compliant, directing her limbs, her hands, her mouth. Yes, he says. Yes, there. She thinks: No, not I. Not you. She thinks: We have moved too far away to touch. Still, she moves through it, his wishes, lies between the arches of his arms, his chest heavy against hers. A foxhole once, a den of safety. Not now. The gale finds her, the light and space. Even when she cries out. She closes her eyes, reaches beyond the sounds of the bed, the rhythm of flesh, stretches, away from the orange light of shuttered eyelids, away from Nate, into herself, beyond herself. Holds there, rigid, teetering. Squeezes her eyes to shut out that face: that nose, those eyes, that black-haired blue boy. Jumps

127

Jesus, Penny, Nate says, peeling away from her. Jesus. I guess we needed that.

She thinks: Yes. She thinks: And yet. Not together, even now. She sinks back into the bed, listens to the steady emptying of adrenaline, the pulse hammering in her ears quieting, slowing. She thinks: Still the hollow.

Nate's breathing slows, deepens. Lovely surprise, his mouth says, thick, heavy with sleep. Lovely, lovely. When his mouth relaxes Pen rolls away, curls up her knees, angles the bedside light. Reaches for the book.

No, she thinks. Not I. Not still. Not me.

There's nothing except through yourself. Hold onto this phrase. Keep it close, a mantra. A key to yourself. They are Ernest's words, but you can turn them against him. If you are his creature, his golem, then this could be your breath, the scrap of text in your mouth, your life-giving line. Repeat the words, in the night, in the darkness of the hotel bedroom, David asleep, Ernest absent. Will yourself to continue. The words keep you awake. Say them. Feel them on your tongue.

Nothing except through yourself. Nothing. Yourself. Except.

What did David say, when you made this pronouncement? Something about not needing to try, not needing to immortalize yourself. You think, that's rich, coming from a writer. But Ernest understands. You know this because of the speeches he gives you. You talk well, even if you don't get to write yourself. It is, you say, like being hungry all the time. You cannot create; cannot write or paint. But you want to make something. You cannot bear for the world to exist without forming it anew somehow, taking it into yourself and shaping it and breathing it out again. Is that what they do, David, Ernest? Are creative acts mere excretions? Exhalations? But no. That is not what you mean. What you mean is that experience, that landscape, that being and moving in the physical stuff of the world, fill you with insatiability. It's not that you are insatiable, you say. You are easily sated. Ernest made you that way. It is a medal David wears proudly, his ability to satisfy you. No. This is an appetite that cannot be sated. It is a hunger that feeds itself and grows ever greater.

If Ernest will not let you write or paint, perhaps he will give you a child. But already you know that will not be. Ernest does not intend for you to be fruitful. What would it mean for him, he who made you? How would it be if you were to go on without him, turn your own clay?

No: he is the creator. You ask for too much.

Fine, you say. You do not say it out loud. You do not stamp your feet. You hold it down: yes, you behave yourself. Anger makes you stronger, remember? Rage, humiliation, shame. They are good for you.

You are in the cafe in Madrid. See the fountains in the square. Hear the play of water. David is opposite you. Look at him. Feel the weight of his disappointment, his disapproval. He does not like your changes. In bed, yes: then they are for pleasure, for play. He can cope with your whims as long as they are secret. But in the daylight, in a public space? No. He will not tolerate it, will not be party to it. He walked away from you this morning. Left you alone and took his remorse to a cafe. You found him there, drinking absinthe. When you saw him, the sickly green tinge to his cheeks, the crease between his brows, you knew. You have outgrown him. You were made to please him but his need sickens you.

Look at him. See the sullen pout of his lip. You made the changes again in the night and today you walked in the clear hot sun and the cool shaded gallery and you were a boy. You played at being a boy as best you could. For a while you convinced yourself. Remember the liberty of it, this otherness, this anonymity. You walked as a boy and when men saw you, your shape, your clear eyes, your proud cheekbones, your sun-darkened skin, your close-cropped hair, they were cowed. They did not covet. Your limbs were long and straight, your tread light. Feel that surety, that proprietorial arrogance. The world was yours. You strode through it without molestation. Every glance you drew was turned aside by your aura of entitlement, of your absolute right to be.

Is that what it is like to be a man? No wonder you do not want to be a woman.

Every time you make a change you move further away. Good. David thinks you are doing it to be like him, to become him. Let him think that. Let him think you want to have matching hair, matching skin, to be two halves of one smooth shell. Every time you do it – shorten your hair, bleach it, tan your skin – you shave away a little more of how you were made. You grow into yourself, toward yourself. To him, David, Ernest, you are a figure retreating. David thinks this is a symptom of madness.

You are never going back. Are you? You will never be like the others.

Ernest is losing control of you. So he turns away and begins again elsewhere. He believes that if he neglects you, withdraws his energy, you will shrivel, shrink, become passive again. Then he can handle you as he wishes.

He couldn't be more wrong.

6.

Pen waits at her desk. She moves papers from one pile to another, straightens books on shelves, stares at emails. The clock on the phone says 11.05. He is late. She rests her hands on her knees, pulse heavy in each fingertip. She shivers. 11.06. She thinks: He is not coming. She thinks: It doesn't matter to him. Why should it matter? She thinks: Well then. Make coffee. Leave. Anything. Do something.

The screen before her shifts: a message. From Max. So, she thinks. Cancelling. She clicks on the line, mouth dry, reads it from the corner of an eye.

Dear Penelope, I am still on the bus but nearly there. I am so so sorry. Please can you wait for me? I will understand if you need to be somewhere else. Really so sorry to be late. Max

Pen springs up, paces, leaves the office, leaves the door open, stalks along the corridor to the staffroom. Stands empty-handed in the kitchen. Stares at the taps. Runs the cold water and puts her wrists beneath the hard stream. She thinks: Ice, calm, breathe. She thinks: Penelope. He is on his way. He is coming closer, every minute closer, and he will be here. Soon he will. The campus. The corridor. The office. The insanity of waiting. She thinks: Let him come, let him be gone again, let it be over. Pulling a tooth. Falling on a sword. Nothing worse than the waiting and then it is done and nothing can alter it whatever happens.

She walks back to her office, sits at the desk. 11.14. Then the knock and he comes in, Max O'Grady, red-cheeked, unwinding a long scarf, puffing.

I am so sorry, he says.

It's fine, she says. Sit down, get your breath back.

He puts down his satchel, shrugs off his coat, closes the door.

Thank you, he says. For waiting. And for agreeing to supervise me. You probably think I'm really pushy but I so wanted to write about this book.

It's not a problem, she says. How are your ideas shaping up?

He digs into his satchel and fishes out notebook, pen, his copy of the novel, the faded library hardback lacking its dust jacket, foxed and frayed. She watches him move, watches his hands, the nails short and neat, the knuckles swollen with cold, fine dark hairs spreading like roots from his wrists.

He talks about the book, about the essay, about David as Hemingway, about the writer's paradise shattered by the outside world. About articles he has read that tell him publication of the book was a travesty, a crime against Hemingway's intentions.

But Max, she says, we cannot know his intentions. All we have is the book in front of you.

He leans forward, knee bouncing. What about his manuscript? Max says. So much was cut.

Do you have the manuscript? she asks.

Well, he says. I mean—

All we have to go on is the book, she says. It isn't everything Hemingway wrote. It's a distilled version of a great sprawling collection of ideas. It might not begin as he wanted it to – it probably doesn't end as he would have ended it. But it is what we have. It must stand. So start with that.

Max nods, clicks the lid of his pen against his lips. She watches, looks away: window screen shelf desk phone. 11.34. Anything but Max O'Grady's mouth, swell of lip, tapping, opening.

There's something else, he says. Connected to this. I wanted to ask you about it.

Yes?

In Dr Saunders' class last term we talked about whether there should still be a place for Hemingway. In the canon. You know, because of his opinions? But now I'm thinking you will say— just stick to the book itself. That his life doesn't matter.

She thinks: Safety in debate. A proffered gauntlet. Feels herself sink back into the seat, shoulders unknotting, fingers unlacing.

What do you think, Max? Does it matter?

Max frowns. Part of me thinks yes, he says. I've been reading a Hemingway biography and he was— Well. He used racist language and bullied his wives. He turned on his friends.

Yes, says Pen. Some of his work includes unpleasant language and attitudes of the time. His letters show he was jealous and unstable. He lashed out, made enemies, threatened violence. We can talk about that, if it interests you. It has interested plenty of biographers.

So should I write about that too?

That's up to you, she says. What do you want to be your focus? Do you want to write about Hemingway's work as still relevant today? Do you want to prove that it isn't? Or do you want to see where the book takes you first?

Max shrugs. I don't know. I guess I need to start with the book, like you said.

Pen nods. She thinks: Too harsh? She thinks: Do not shut him down. He is right to question. Hemingway the brute

Hemingway the brawler. What of Hemingway the damaged, the deranged, the despairing? Does Steve Saunders mention *him* in class? She thinks: No matter. Max is bright. Let him find his own way of reading.

Let's go back to *The Garden of Eden* for now, she says. What draws you to this text? What do you see in it?

Conflict, says Max. Confusion. Self-doubt.

Interesting.

Max leans into his notebook, writes the words in narrow, oblique capitals. *CONFLICT CONFUSION SELF-DOUBT.* Hovers his pen under the last; underlines it once. Twice.

Good, she says. What else? What do these responses suggest to you?

Max's pen twitches, ticking clicking between long fingers.

We talked about it last time, he says. If Hemingway is like David, then maybe he isn't this macho stereotype after all. Maybe there are things he wants, really wants, though he feels he shouldn't.

Okay, she says, to his flicking pen, the notebook, the folded seam of denim beneath it. That's a beginning, she says.

So I need to start again, Max says. With that?

With whatever the text reveals to you. A hermeneutic treatment: no biographies, no critiques. Not yet. Read the novel straight through, she says, then read it again. It is short enough. Make notes on anything that strikes you. Anything. Make a list. Don't worry about a direction, because that will reveal itself. The associations will come. Lists are wonderful like that.

Do I have time? he says. I mean, shouldn't I be writing up by now?

You have plenty of time, she says. You have the holidays to get started. Just make sure you have some ideas to bring next time, a rough plan. Or email me, if it helps.

Really? he says. I mean, is that okay?

Of course. And if the list doesn't work for you, brainstorm your ideas, sketch them out, see if anything joins up. When you have a theme you want to pursue we can shape some questions around it. Then you have a narrower line of enquiry, which is what you need. Otherwise the book and everything you bring to it is wide open, and you'll have trouble containing your argument.

Thanks, Max says.

Okay, she says.

She thinks: There. It is done. No danger.

This thing, he says. With the book being part of something else. Something bigger, like a piece of the writer's life, inner and outer. Or a part of the manuscript version. It's a metaphor in itself, isn't it?

How do you mean? she says.

Max stretches, frowns. I mean, it's like Hemingway's iceberg, he says. The thing you said in that lecture about how much he showed, and how much he hid in his writing. It's as if the book, this book, is the bit we get to see, and the rest is below the surface.

That's one way you could look at it, she says. But without seeing the rest, you can only speculate.

He nods. I like it as an idea though. It's like the manuscript is a person too, you know, the whole of a self? And the book is the part we are allowed to see.

Yes, she says. The surface doesn't reveal much backstory. The layers and omissions and history we can touch upon but never directly encounter.

He glances at the floor, a gathering.

That's the thing about meeting someone, he says. The part we see is just a fraction and the excitement comes from finding out about the rest, the mass under the surface.

Or of making guesses, Pen says.

Isn't that what we do? he says. I mean, we have an idea of someone and hope we are right about them.

I suppose so. Although people do reveal themselves. But it takes time to really know someone else, and even then one can be surprised.

And yet, he says, sometimes you meet someone and you feel like you already know them. I mean, as if you can understand things about them without being told.

She looks away again. 11.42. She thinks: Does he know what he is doing? Is he really doing it?

Perhaps, she says, we just make it up. We fashion people as we want them to be.

Yes, Max says, blinking. If they don't let us see for sure.

Pen's throat closes. Well, she says. It is a croak, a whisper. Perhaps you can use these thoughts in the essay somehow. See what you can detect from the book itself though. The book comes first.

She thinks: Treacherous body. Do not give me away.

She thinks: And what of his ideas of me? Mine of him?

She thinks: I do not want to be an idea.

Well, he says.

Well, she says.

I guess I won't see you again before Christmas, he says.

Probably not, Pen says. I've got my last seminar in an hour.

I've finished now, he says.

Well then, she says.

He gathers his things, loops the strap of satchel over one hand. Sits, looks at her. Waits. She thinks: Let him go. Do not get up. Do not.

Have a nice holiday, he says.

Thanks, she says. You too. And good luck with the assignment.

I may email you then, he says.

That's fine, if you need to.

Yes.

He looks at his hands, at the floor.

Max, she says. You can go now.

Yes, he says. But I really don't want to.

And there it is. She closes her mouth against it, bites down hard. Max looks up, eyes raking, anxious.

Last time, he says. I mean, when I was last here, we—

Max, she says. It's all right. But I do think you should go.

Please, he says. Please don't ask me to.

He drops the satchel strap and reaches over to her, touches her hair, her neck, fingers trembling. She thinks: So this is it then. This is how. And he. Not me. He.

I love your hair like this, he says. I can see more of your face.

You must go, Max, she says.

Please don't say that.

We can't, she says. I need you to go.

Are you sure? he says. Why?

Because I won't be able to push you away.

Oh, he says.

Pen stands and he rises to meet her and they stretch into each other, mouths meeting, limbs colliding.

I wasn't sure, he says, to her ear, to her cheek. I was afraid it was just me, a stupid crush.

We cannot, she says, to his neck, the blackness of his hair. Sinks in her fingers.

I hoped, he says. But I felt such an idiot.

Surely, she says. How could you not know? But we cannot.

We can, he says. Please.

She thinks: Stop. We must stop. Stop while we still can.

Pen steps back, untangles, holds his face. Max O'Grady's face, lids heavy over blue, mouth open. Kisses him again, sucks in his tongue, feels him lean into her. Tips him gently away.

Enough now, she says. Enough.

He nods, breathes. Smiles. Thank you, he says. Thank you thank you thank you.

You know we cannot work together, Pen says. Not like this.

Don't, he says. Please. Nobody will know.

She laughs. They will, she says. They will only need to look at me.

He laughs too, scoops her chin, kisses her mouth, cheeks, ears. Not enough, he says. More. More please.

Go, she says. While I can still say it.

He does: takes his things and opens the door and turns, grins, leaves.

Pen stands, sways, hand at mouth, stunned. Tastes him on her fingers.

~

Climbing the college steps she feels the change. She is taller than she was yet smaller, lighter. The soles of her feet ache against the concrete. Her knees bend like springing traps. She blinks and sees him, blinks to see him, a miracle of photons impressing his face, keeping him always in view.

She stumbles through the final seminar, the students bouncing, restive, dogs sensing a storm. She finishes early and joins some of them in the bar. Mulled wine, mince pies, a giant screen littered with grinding bodies, voices silenced by the jukebox in the corner. She half-listens, smiles, crosses and uncrosses legs, her body singing, chest shouting, touching glass to lips to feel the shock of contact, her own tongue a swollen organ of want filling her mouth.

~

It is with her for days. The shock, the craving. It changes everything. Nate and Toby are ghosts in fog. Everything reminds her of him: a single boot in the doorway, an empty mug, the hungry arches between gateposts. She cannot move without feeling the press of clothes against her, cannot sit without the weight of him pushing her chest. In the night she lies awake, dry-eyed, staring, willing it not to be so. She is terrified. In the mornings her lips are raw, desiccated.

Christmas. End-of-term meetings, department party, five weeks of waiting. Pen is an exile, escaping back to campus at every excuse. She leaves Nate and Toby Christmas shopping and returns to the office just to be there, to breathe there. Wishing it back again, wishing it away. Five weeks. And nothing to be done.

She works through the days, kicks against them to stay afloat. There are visits, friends, presents are wrapped and unwrapped, meals cooked and eaten. She tries to be there, to weigh the days, to remember their purpose. She hugs Toby, squeezes Nate's arm, smiles, smiles, smiles. Distance changes everything: guilt, jealousy, recrimination, fear, anger, rejection. She tastes each one slowly.

She tries to picture Max's face but now it will only come in small patches, images in close-up, the view through a child's telescope. She thinks: Did I dream him? She thinks: Too much, too suddenly, and now he is in retreat.

No word from him. A week. Two. She holds her breath. Nothing. She thinks: It never was. He does not care. She thinks: It was nothing, nothing. She thinks: How else could it be? She thinks: I must tell him. I am here and it can be and we must let it. How? She thinks: Too easy. I have made it too easy for him. She thinks: We cannot. What if I am wrong?

She pictures Max with his family, friends from his home town (where? who? she knows so little of him) nights out, drinking, boasting, swapping stories of college conquests. Would he tell anyone about her? Would he brag? Or joke? Is she a drunken anecdote now? She thinks: How could I expose myself to this? A moment's indiscretion, that's all it would take. Toby, career, friends, home, self: collapsing into each other, lost to her. And for what? A vain infatuation, a boy, a rush of weakness.

And yet. Max shaking, touching her neck. She thinks: What if it is real? What if it does mean something? His wolf grin, elated. Because of her. Because he had wanted and so had she. She thinks: Is that so terrible? She thinks: Yes. How could it not be?

A morning, three weeks in, the sky bright, the frost thick on the grass, the air sharp, and she wakes, moves around the house and realises that something has lifted. She walks from one room to the next and the dread is gone. She thinks: Why not? Embrace it. She thinks: Why would he pretend? Why should he not want her? She has been wanted before. She thinks: Anything we can have. Do what we can. See? she asks herself. See how it feels to accept it? Accept it, a gift, a handsel. Anything we can do. It doesn't have to be nothing.

The fourth week. With the waiting she becomes irrational, irascible. Everything irritates: Nate's burnt toast scrapings, Toby's pyjamas balled up and thrown in the corner, toothpaste on the bathroom mirror. Small labours, fast undone by others. Marking, marking. Her patience paper-thin. She cannot work: Stein is lost to her again. Her book is a sprawling coastline, her concentration a rudderless tub. One night she is driven from the house by it, stands in the hard tight air of the garden, gasping, fingernails screwing into palms. A neighbour's dog barks, barks, barks. She thinks: I will explode. If I do not see him. If he does not write.

The next morning, an email: Max. Pen opens it, terrified, furtive, euphoric. No subject, just a quote from the Hemingway novel. Catherine's haircut.

The lines of her cheekbones showed clear as he had never seen them before and she smiled and her face was heartbreaking.
M x

She reads it, rereads it, speaks it aloud. An answer. A declaration.

All morning it plays in her head. She busies herself in the house, removing holiday traces, packing away, setting things in order. Nate drives Toby to a friend's house, fidgeting out the final days before school. Now she has precious time alone: to breathe, to reason, to find the right response. How? She sweeps spent pine needles from floorboards, tips them into the fireplace. The book as a code. She thinks: A dialogue written between lines. Invisible ink. She thinks: Careful now. Careful what you choose. So many ways of reading, of seeing.

She thumbs through the Hemingway book. There is a place she recalls, a line: David writing the hardest story he can think of, the story he has always known must be written. Pen finds the place: Chapter Twelve, the second book. She thinks: Perhaps. This could be it.

To write his story, David must set aside everything else. He puts away the narrative of his days with Catherine, closes off the creeping chaos of Marita's presence. The story has been a long time coming. It is the shadow in the corner of his eye. He must write it. But how? It is impossible. It can never be done. He finishes one story and puts away the notebook, pushes himself up from the desk, paces. He goes out to the room he shares with his wife and finds the note and car key she has left him. He thinks of driving and meeting Catherine and this new girl and the weight of everything presses into him again. But writing will shut it out: writing shuts everything out. He comes back to his desk, begins the story, sets out the first passage. The impossibility of the story smooths itself out and he is in the writing, beyond the room, away from everything.

Pen is there. She feels the wood of the desk warming under David's notebook, hears the hush of pencil lead on paper. Feels David turn himself out, probing, scouring, finding the place of the story and unpacking it. But there is always the distance, the voice that is not his own, the thing that makes the writing fly.

See? he tells himself. How simple it is to do the impossible. How quickly we undo ourselves. She thinks: Max will understand this, surely? An acceptance. The story is impossible to write but David writes it anyway. Nothing is really impossible. There is always a chance it will write itself.

She opens Max's email, copies the line from the book into a reply. Reads it. Deletes it. Writes it again.

Dear Max,
You see how simple what you cannot do is?
Penelope

Presses Send.

She thinks: Hear me. Understand me. She thinks: Semaphore. Signalling from hilltops. She thinks: I am a madwoman, waving my arms in the wind.

She cannot wait now. She cannot be in the house, wondering, regretting, analysing. She leaves a scribbled note, puts on a coat, walks into town. The air bites her bare neck. She pulls up her collar, flattens it again. Any sensation is a pleasure, her body hungry, leaning into the wind. *Her face was heartbreaking.* Her face. Pen's face.

~

Pen steers through crowds, shop doorway jingles, sale signs, giant sequined snowflakes. Incongruous festive decorations, the last party guests who will not leave. It is January. Two weeks more. Ten days perhaps. Will he come to her straight away? Will he return early? She thinks: It could be soon. Today is

Wednesday. By Monday the library will be open again, the campus reviving, the home students trickling back in. She has a planning meeting. Administrators will be at their desks. The buses will run. The bars will open. She thinks: It could be a week. It could be. He may.

She sees it in the faces of strangers reflecting back at her. Anticipation. Excitement. She looks away, a guilty child, thoughts colouring her face. And yet shining with it. She thinks: How could they not see? She thinks: Max O'Grady wants me. No wonder people stare. No wonder I draw attention.

She finds herself in a coffee shop, steam on the windows, screaming espresso machines. Janis Joplin faintly wailing. She orders, carries tray to table, sits, stares absently at the counter. A man in the queue turns, tall, white-haired, locks eyes, smiles. Pen smiles back. He takes his drink, sits at a table across from her, removes his jacket. Walks past to collect a newspaper, sits again. Pen sips, scalds her lip, snatches the cup away. She unwraps a square of chocolate and places it on her tongue, lets it rest there, sliding thickly, coating the roof of her mouth. On the chair beside her a fleck of something white: she picks it up. Paper. Origami. A white scrap folded into the shape of a tiny bird, two points for feet. She stands it on the table. Was it there before? She feels eyes on her: the man again, watching. She holds up the paper bird, a question. He shrugs, smiles, wrinkles in the corners of his eyes, round pleasant face, carefully tailored beard. Fifty, more maybe. A warm face. A face to fall in love with. She thinks: If I were looking. She thinks: I have forgotten how to look. She thinks: Is this his? Does it mean something? She holds the bird again, feels the sharp creases with her thumb. A signal of sorts. An omen. She puts it in her pocket, blows on her coffee, circles spreading, lapping the broad rim of the cup. Above it the man watches, following her small movements, taking her in. How long since a man looked at her that way? She cannot remember.

She cannot remember ever being like this.

You can talk to him now: him, Ernest. Ignore David. David is only doing what Ernest tells him to do. He is a weak point of access. You will try your own way.

You know where Ernest is. Tell him that you know he is at his desk just as you have seen David at his, and that he is writing you, now, his pencil scratching paper. Tell him that you know him because he made you and because he made David in his image and you have exhausted David.

You tell him to take you beyond this man that he shaped from parts of himself and this bed made from all the beds he has been in and wanted to be in and this hotel that once meant something to him. Tell him that you want to touch the hand that moves across the page; that you want his hand to move across you, not through David but of itself. That he made you this way and that you are his, not David's. You tell him that you know he is listening.

How do you know?

David's hand was reaching for your hair, inches from your ear. His fingers do not flex. The air does not move. The breeze from the sea that lifted the blind is caught; it hangs above your head, filling the fabric like a thumb pressed into wax. Nothing stirs.

The pencil hovers. Ernest is listening.

Something snaps. Pencil lead? A chair scrapes. It is not in the room, not this room. Did he hear you? Is he there? You cannot feel him. He has gone. He must have heard you.

He leaves you there, unfinished, unanswered—

7.

Spring term, a great iron gate swinging open.

Pen makes coffee, sits at her desk, stares at the screen. Monday. One more day and she will see him. The square on her calendar is highlighted, the time, 11 a.m., blocked in red. TUTORIAL, MAX O'GRADY.

She thinks through the messages of the past week, lines of text passing between them. Flashes of feeling, questions, promises. All played out in Hemingway's words. And when she sees him at last? She wants to be sure of him. She wants to devour him. She looks at the last message, a simple confirmation of their meeting, laden with unspoken meaning. *11 a.m.*, Max says. *I promise to be on time.* She studies the office, listens to its beat, its eccentricities. The low growl of generator feeding the central heating. The clicking of loose carpet tiles in the corridor outside. Freddie stirring in his cell next door; chair creaking, tap running, strip light buzzing. She thinks: We will never be alone. Max and Penelope. He and I. She thinks: As well. Although. If we.

The afternoon sun is low, sharp, slicing across her papers, her lap. She rises to twist down the blind, shut it out. She thinks: Some privacy then. Whose window might look into hers? What could be seen? Max is tall. If they stood by the desk, kissing, coupling, who might make them out? She opens the blinds again, peers across to the far building, the distant slates of windows.

She thinks: Paranoia. She thinks: Never too careful.

The trees opposite are bare, overgrown, scraping at the far wall. Estates will need to come out, lop branches, use ladders. She pinches herself.

She thinks: Vigilance. She thinks: I have lost all perspective.

Her reply to Max is calm, businesslike. She wants to say: I have been living in a wasteland without you. She wants to say: Come now, I need you. She wants to say: Let me taste you again. She does not say these things. Instead she writes: *Don't forget to bring all notes and a rough plan with you to the tutorial.*

She signs it with her official flourish: full name, title, office hours, address.

Something moves quickly across the desk, black over white. She looks down and sees it: an earwig, twisting its body towards her. She stands and opens the window, scoops up the insect and rolls it into her palm. When she lifts her hand the earwig rights itself, scuttles across the soft pad of skin, makes for the open cuff of her sleeve. She thinks: It walks here as it would on any surface. Unaware, unalarmed, without intention. She tips the creature through the gap to the path below. Farewell, little one. Looks up at the windows opposite again, closes her own, snaps blinds. Freddie Mann coughs next door. She thinks: We are all just inhabiting spaces, finding a place and then another, another. Moving between cells.

~

Tuesday, 11 a.m. Max O'Grady strides in, shuts the door, gathers her wordlessly. Tips her head back and opens her mouth with his tongue.

When he leaves she stands at the desk, shaking out her hands to quiet them. Looks long at the face hanging in the darkened monitor before her. It is not her face, does not belong there. The phone rings: she holds the receiver.

She cannot speak. Her mouth, compacted, has forgotten how else to express itself.

~

It goes on like this: tutorials without substance, without text. Every second or third day they meet. Twenty minutes of furtive, famished kissing. Ten minutes. Five, when Pen has a seminar to teach and he will not leave. She stumbles between rooms, desire fogging movement. Finally she tells him they must stop, must talk, must focus. His long essay is due in three weeks. They need to think of that.

Yes, he says, hands on her knees, thighs. Yes. But you must let me see you. And not just like this.

She thinks: Like what? She says, How else can we be?

Meet me one evening, he says. Anywhere. Please.

How? she says.

He shrugs at the walls, the window, the door that anyone might knock on. Anyhow, he says. So long as we can really be alone. He kisses her again, leaning long against her.

No, she says, you need to go. I've got to teach.

Christ, he says. Rubs hard against her leg. Have some mercy, please.

Go, she says. Go go go go go.

~

153

She finds a way: a Friday, Nate home for once to see to Toby. Pen pleads duty, an external examiner who must be met with, dined, entertained. She showers, scrubs, dresses, perfumes. Leaves them both slumping, telly on. Returns to wait in her office, blinds drawn, table lamp lowered, door ajar. Listens for telling knocks in the stillness of the corridor. Checks for darkness in staffroom, kitchen. Administrators linger in corridors, leave in clusters; Freddie Mann bustles past them waving car keys, calling out goodbyes. By seven the building is quiet, the ominous thud of generator breaking waves across silence. Finally Pen leaves her office, strains against the *thuck* of closing door, locks it softly behind her. Circles the building, seeking strips of light beyond closed blinds. The windows within are dark. The windows of the building opposite are dark. Thin February rain: a blank wall.

She shivers, retraces. Unlocks and enters her office. Sits at the desk, smooths her skirt. Waits.

He arrives, breathless, colour high. His walk is different. She thinks: Does he doubt it, now? But still he smiles, mouth skewed, closes the door gently. She comes towards him, past him, locks the door, leans into it.

Are we safe? he asks, a whisper.

I think so.

He watches her. Takes off his coat, scarf. Sits on the perilous edge of a seat and removes his shoes. Socks.

Wet, he says. Sorry.

Oh well, she says.

She crosses to the desk again, leans into the hard edge, feels the balls of her feet pushing, rising her up.

And you, he says, to her feet, to the floor beneath her.

She bends, unzips boots, rolls down stockings, kicks them aside.

Here, he says. Come here.

She goes to him, stands, stoops, rests her knees against his. Inside his.

This is crazy, she says.

Yes, he says. And very, very horny.

Pen laughs. Covers her mouth. Kisses him.

They stumble at first, feeling through clothes, between them, beneath. She thinks: Ridiculous garments, upholstery, *a necessary waist*. They stand, teeter, seeking purchase against walls, bookshelves, ledges. Gasping, shedding, unbuttoning unclasping. Max pulls away, shrugs pooled jeans from ankles, kicks them from him. Bends to feel inside a pocket. Holds up a small square of silver.

She thinks: Good. Savvy boy. She thinks: I didn't think this through. Was it denial? She thinks: Nothing beyond chance. She watches him remove his shorts, remove her skirt, pull at her, treading down the layers. He kneels, parts her flesh with his fingers. His tongue reaches and she sways, barks sharply, falls back, cold steel of filing cabinet against thigh, want surging, arching her toes to points. Faint metallic ripping, his hands fast, a smoothing down and he stands, pushes at her thighs, lifts into her.

When they are done she dresses quickly. He is languorous, easy, taking his time over shirt buttons, smiling, wry. She thinks: Pert youth. Oh for an ounce of it. His courage. His certainty.

They sit for a while, silent, feeling each other's hands. Testing, exploring. He kisses her fingers, sucks them one by one.

You, he says. Just as I'd hoped you would be.

Likewise, she says.

He laughs.

A click — the faintest breath of it, beyond the door. They freeze.

Was—

She stops his mouth shakes her head holds her breath. The clicking shifts, moves, separates. She thinks: The loose carpet tiles. Outside. Corridor. Somebody. Listening.

They wait. At last the soft shutting of the far door. Pen removes her hand. Max swallows.

Who? he says.

She says, Who knows?

She thinks: What difference does it make? Somebody. Anybody. Somebody heard. She thinks: This is it. Karma. There will be retribution.

Hey, Max says, hand on her cheek. Hey, don't worry. It was just someone walking past. A cleaner. They probably didn't hear us. Why would anyone be listening?

She shrugs. Feels the sinking sickness, a settling stone inside her.

Don't, he says. Please. We've waited so long for this.

She thinks: Long? Waited? She thinks: And yet, yes. An age. A thousand chapters of waiting. She tries to smile, tries to stay with him. He pulls her closer, kisses growing heavy, hands urgent. She thinks: Again? She thinks: Of course. She thinks: I had forgotten this, the appetite of youth, of novelty.

She shakes her head. She cannot, not now. That click of carpet a flicking switch, all wants extinguished. She pictures Toby's face, his frown of concentration. She turns away, tries not to retch. Somebody. Somebody heard them.

She stands, hovers, unsteady, her ears feeling the air, straining for tremors. She steps backwards, switches on the desk lamp, blinks into the sudden disc of light. Their breath against the hum of the room, his shape pale in seeping fluorescent light from the corridor, flashing clock figures. She seeks him in that space, his narrow calves, his knees.

Time to go, she says.

~

Pen locks the office door behind her. Washes in the hand basin of the staffroom toilet, hands shaking, thighs bruised, pats paper towels between her legs.

Driving home she tries to think only of Max, the taste of him, his quick animal noises. She switches on the radio: eleven o'clock headlines. Turns it off. She thinks: Last orders. *Hurry up please it's time.* She thinks: I could use a drink. She thinks: Toby will be in bed now. Even Nate wouldn't let him stay up so late.

Nate. She waits for the hammer blow. It does not fall. The shock comes only from not thinking of him, from the slow dawning of not having thought of him at all.

1954: Africa

He shifted his swollen arm a little. It sent the fire straight
through his back again. Christ, it hurt. The ringing in his ears
had toned down at least. When he wrote the Cuban book for
Marty he'd given his rum-running hero Harry a shot to the
stomach. Harry lay on the deck and tried to be still. The trick
was not to move or drink any water. Christ, he felt like Harry.
Every time the boat tossed he had to bite his lip. He didn't
want to keep shouting out. He didn't want his wife running in
every five minutes expecting to find him dead.

Well, they'd already taken him for dead. He'd been sitting
up in bed on the crossing reading the obituaries. Those sons of
bitches couldn't wait for him to go. Two plane crashes made a
good story. The papers loved it. Then he was back in Nairobi
and very much alive. He wasn't some skinned and mounted
trophy to hang on the wall. He was indestructible. He had
been blown up and shot at and pulled out of wrecks, and he'd
stood in front of a charging lion. He'd even fallen into a brush
fire. Oh, they liked that too. But as soon as he was gone the
biographers would be all over him, picking at his carcass. Well,
the bastards could wait.

Kittner had left him a large gin and tonic and he sipped it
carefully. So what if the doctor said no? Doctors always said no.
He had been covered in ointment and bandaged and hooked
up to tubes, but now he was settled in the cabin and apart from
his back he felt fine. He wanted to feel fine. His eyes were

blurry and he'd been groggy from the drugs but that was all cleared away. He had the sharpness and clearness that he'd felt at the front when he was lying in a ditch being raked by machine-gun fire. There was nothing like being shot at to purify the emotions and give you a sense of purpose. His head was buzzing with the things he could write and the things he had started on. He had a game plan now. Four years ago they'd said he was all washed up. They tore apart his Venice book. That didn't stop him. They talked about him like he was some kind of fossil they'd already tagged and put on a dusty shelf somewhere. To hell with that. He had hunkered down in his tower at the Finca and given them the story of the fisherman and his giant marlin and they lapped it up. Some of the bastards sniped about him and called him a boor and a bar brawler. Some of them dragged up how much they hated the Venice book. But none of them could say a damned thing about the fishing story that could touch him. He knew it was good. Kittner said it was so good it absolved him of all sins. Christ, they gave him the Pulitzer for it. There was even talk about the Nobel.

He was like the old fisherman. They could rob him but they couldn't kill him. He wouldn't lay down for anyone.

He sipped his gin. A hell of a trip it had been. They had left Cuba back in the summer and sailed to France and gone by road to Paris. They dropped the kit for Africa in the basement of the Ritz and spent some time in the usual places. He'd thought about the Venetian girl but it didn't hurt like before. His hide was toughening with age. He and Kittner took a car down to the south and spent some time on the beaches. Down in the Riviera he was filled with ideas for the novel about the young American writer. He had left the case with the scripts in it back home in a vault but he made notes and added some chapters. He was filling the book out again, now, in his head. His arm was too swollen and his back too sore to write but his head was clear enough to think.

Before they left for the trip he and Kittner had spent long weeks on the beaches of the island Paraíso. They took *Pilar* out there and anchored her off the lee side of the island. There were palms and pines and the coral reef kept the waters warm. They fished and cooked the fish on campfires. They walked and swam without suits and talked and listened to the radio. That was how they'd found out about the Pulitzer. They were close to home but nobody had found them and there was no mail, just the two of them and Gregorio for the cooking and keeping the boat, and so it was the first he'd heard of it. He'd been talking to Gregorio about their catch and he came back to find Kittner standing up and smiling at him and waving for him to come closer.

Listen, Papa! she said. Listen! The radio! They are talking about you.

He huffed and swatted his hand at the air. What are those bastards saying about me now? he said. Do they want to crucify me again?

Oh Papa, she said. Oh no. They want to immortalize you.

He wasn't ready for that yet, but he'd take the prize money all the same.

He shifted on the bed and felt behind him for the cushions. The pain pitched up from his kidneys and into his shoulders and he let it out in a low growl. He pinched at a cushion and eased it down behind him so it pushed into his spine. The pressure was good and when he sat back into the bunched-up cushion it was like floating. Even though his back was shot to pieces just thinking about the island disturbed and excited him. He would use this feeling in his novel. Paraíso was a piece of Eden and he and Kittner were close and happy there. He would give his young American writer that time on his own beaches in the South of France and then he would take it away from him.

On the trip they had gone along from the coast and into Spain and seen the running of the bulls at Pamplona and some of the fights. The bullfights had lost none of their drama but he was sickened to see how poorly some of the matadors made their kills. They were sloppy and the bulls suffered too much. Then they went back to Paris and swapped their gear around and took the ship to Mombasa.

Africa always had something to teach you. He knew there would be material there but until now he hadn't grasped its different uses. There was the safari piece he had promised for the magazine. The magazine had sent a photographer. Kittner was furious because she had wanted to write the piece herself and get paid for it but of course they had offered him the job. He had written that piece about the safari and the plane crashes and he was glad it was done and not hanging over him still. He had another story shaping up that could become a long story like the fisherman and the giant marlin, or perhaps there would be enough for a novel. But there was something else that had happened and he found now, sitting with his burns and his tortured back and his sudden clarity, sipping his gin, that he could use it for the book about the young American writer.

He had been on the safari to shoot animals. Old Percival, his guide from twenty or more years ago, came out of retirement to take them out and find them quarry. Percival lined him up a rhino and a leopard but he had little luck with either. In fact he made a bloody mess of it. That was what had changed and he knew he had to use it in his writing.

He let off several shots into the rhino but she didn't go down. They followed the spoor until it started to get dark but they couldn't find her. When they found her the next day she was dead.

He lay awake in the tent after shooting the rhino and listened to the night sounds. Kittner lay on her back snoring. Her breath stirred part of the mosquito net hanging above them. He thought about the rhino and her small black eyes and the way they seemed to shrink and narrow at him before he fired. She was already wounded and it was his job to finish her off. He fired and she kicked about and was gone. He had been an excellent shot ten years ago but his eyes were weak and his shoulders ached. Percival and Kittner had talked around this and told him not to worry and when they got back to camp they made drinks and told stories as if it hadn't happened. But in the tent that night he knew the truth of why he had messed up the kill. The rhino was close and he could smell her and smell the fear and the fury of her cornered there in the scrub and he fired at her and missed. Her hide was old and tough like his. He shot at her but he couldn't bear to hurt her. Years ago his heart had been in the killing and so it was quick and easy for him. Now he felt no pleasure in it and so it was slow and hard.

In the tent in the dark he listened to Kittner snoring and the mosquitoes humming and the small sounds of creatures moving, and he wept. He wept for the rhino dying slowly, alone and at bay. He prayed for her in his way and wished her speedy passing and begged her forgiveness. He never wanted to shoot anything ever again. He was done with killing.

A few days later Percival set him up with a leopard and he and his friend shot at it together. The photographer was there and the magazine people wanted pictures of him shooting and killing. Without speaking of it he let his friend take the killing shot and fired along with him. Then the photographer took a picture of him with the dead leopard. Kittner pointed out that there was no way of telling who had killed it, but he knew. His heart had not been in it. It was not him.

The night after the leopard his friend got very drunk and fell asleep in a chair by the campfire. After a while Kittner went to bed but he sat up with Percival and they drank whiskey from the tin cups. They said very little and looked at the fire.

Forgive me, Percival, he said. I'm a bloody fool.

Percival coughed. Nothing to forgive, old man, he said.

I have no heart for it anymore, he said.

He looked into the fire and into his cup of whiskey but he could not look at Percival.

After a while Percival asked, Is it because of the war?

It is the war, he answered, and it is growing closer to death.

Percival laughed then. I'm nearly seventy, he said. How old are you? Who are you to talk about dying? You have many more years and many more stories to write. Tomorrow you will shoot a lion.

I cannot shoot a lion, he said.

If you cannot I will shoot it for you. There is no shame in that. I will find you a lion, old man. Then we will see.

I would like to find an elephant, he said. But I will only shoot a camera at it.

They laughed then and finished their whiskies and went to bed. Again he lay awake in the night and thought about the rhino. He thought about his mother dying in the ward of an asylum, frightened and raving and not knowing the face of her own daughter. He had sent his sister money for the funeral but he didn't go to see her buried. He thought about his old friend and publisher, Charles Scribner, dying of a heart attack back in New York. He thought about Fife, dying on the operating table with a tumor no one had known about. The night before, he had shouted down the phone at her and hours later she was ill and then she was dead. The shock of it had knocked him so flat he couldn't speak of it and so he toughed it out like it didn't matter. Kittner called him a monster and a cold bastard and in the pit of the black mood that followed he made her suffer and broke things.

It had mattered. Kittner couldn't know it and he couldn't find a way to say it even if she'd listen. There had been so many deaths and he was tired of them. He had maimed the rhino and the rhino had died. He had taken away its dignity and that horrified him.

Sometimes an animal would affect you that way. Now he was in bed on a boat to Italy he felt far enough away from the business with the rhino to make some use of it. He would use it in the novel. The young American writer, David, would write the story of it for him. He would not use the rhino because that would be too close, but he would use the dignity of a great, wounded creature and the shame and horror of destroying it.

He knew now how it would be.

He would have David sitting with his pencils and his note-book in the hotel room in the South of France. There David would craft the story of his childhood in Africa. He sat back hard against the cushions and closed his eyes, the better to tell himself the story.

David is a young boy eager to please his father. His father is a game warden. His father and their guide Juma take the boy ivory hunting. The boy David lies awake in the night and hears the sound of an elephant passing. He and his dog leave the tent and follow the elephant. It is an old bull elephant with great tusks that scrape the ground as he walks. The boy watches the elephant and stays close to him right into the valley. There the elephant circles the skeleton of another elephant.

Yes, he would use that. The game wardens told those stories of animals visiting their dead. It was a good way to trap them. Years ago he'd made the mistake of going back to the old places and finding that everything had changed. But in Africa things did not change. The elephant was lucky that way. But somehow the dead elephant would be a warning. Going back was a kind of death.

He took another drink and thought hard about the elephant skeleton in the valley in the moonlight, the old bull elephant circling and the boy watching. The dead elephant has empty sockets instead of tusks, and the boy understands. The old bull elephant has returned to visit the skeleton of his friend that Juma and the boy's father killed many years before. Or maybe that would come later and Juma would use the dead elephant to trap the old one. Either way, the elephant skeleton gives the boy David a tight feeling in his stomach.

He thought again about the rhino. What was the worst thing that could happen to the boy David? He would need to lose his faith somehow. He would have to betray himself and to be betrayed. Standing watching the elephant in the African night he is just a boy seeing a magnificent creature and feeling sorry for its grief. The boy does not know yet how this will change him.

He had the story now. The next morning the boy David tells his father and Juma about the bull elephant with its huge ivory tusks and they begin to track it. As they follow the dung of the elephant, which gets fresher the closer they get, David comes to learn that he loves the bull elephant and that he is helping to destroy it. There will be no one left to visit the skeleton of the old bull when his carcass has rotted away. His father and Juma find the elephant and kill it. The boy rages and cries and his father is ashamed of him. In the beginning the boy loves and respects his father. Then they kill the old bull elephant and part of that love is lost forever.

He opened his eyes and blinked hard. He had written about a hunter's respect for his quarry in the fisherman story. The old fisherman loved the giant marlin and called him brother, tiring him gently and steadily, finishing him with the harpoon and still loving him as he did so. He had felt like this about some of the fish he had caught, but the feeling about the rhino was new to him. It was such a strong and terrible feeling that he knew he could write it into the story he had planned for the young writer. He knew also that David's wife would be disgusted by the story but that in some way his lover would understand. That was the way it was with people close to you. You never knew if they would get a story or not or if they would think the story was about them. But it wouldn't be about either of the women. It would be about a boy starting to hate his father and finding out about death and shame and betrayal.

His head ached. When he was better he would get into shape. He had lost a lot of weight with the crashes and the sickness but he would build himself up again. Before they left for the trip he had managed his weight and made himself stronger with swimming. It felt good to swim. It was good for his blood pressure too. Every day after writing he would do laps in the pool at the Finca. When he was working on the fisherman story the swimming had helped him to think about water and the sounds it made and to try to understand something of what it meant to be a fish. That sounded crazy but it had helped. He had always been a good swimmer. He enjoyed feeling the weight of water and of pushing it aside with his arms. He liked to dive and he liked to feel the volume of the water against his chest. Often he would swim alone to clear his head. He would swim and the thoughts would come to him and strengthen with each stroke. He would keep them there, holding his breath, letting the ideas come. He liked to swim along the bottom of the pool, and he found the ideas were still there with him when he surfaced.

He had made his young American writer a strong swimmer. Swimming was good for sex. He had remembered that on the island with Kittner. He would see to it that the young writer David had his lover that way too.

Things had never been better between him and his wife. Kittner had always been adventurous in bed and even now she could surprise him. They had explored many things together, especially on Paraíso. There had been new things in Africa too. He was taking that part of Africa home with him to keep, along with the skins and the ivory and the mounted heads. For a long time she'd enjoyed playing at being a boy and making him into her girl. It was not that she wanted other women or that he wanted men, but that they could be those things for each other. Sometimes he was her girl Catherine and she was Peter.

He had already worked those ideas into the novel. When they were in Paris they visited the statues in the Musée Rodin. He took Kittner to see them and she was very moved. She said that she did not want another woman like in one of the statues but that she did want them to become each other, in the way that Rodin's figures were fixed together and carved from the same piece or cast in the same metal. She said that when they were in bed or on the beach of the island they became like that, melded into each other. If anyone saw them together they would not know where one began and the other ended. She wanted it to be like this and to be so that nobody could tell them apart. She wanted to become him and for him to become her.

But I am an old man with a broad chest and white in my beard, he said.

I will make you into a young woman, she said. And I am your boy Peter and I will change for you.

How will you do that? he asked.

In the bed in the hotel in Nairobi she showed him what she meant, lying on top of him and pushing inside him with her thumb and rocking them back and forth together until he cried out.

Afterwards he called her the prince of devils and she said he was her angel. A hairy angel, he said. She laughed and asked him to write it out for her so she could keep it always. He wrote in her journal about the changes they had made and how happy they had been about it and then he signed his name underneath.

~

He shifted in the bed again. It didn't matter how cut up and burned and battered he was, he couldn't help how that made him feel. He would tell Kittner about it when she came in. He would tell her how Mr Scrooby felt about it.

It could all go into the novel but it would be a different kind of Eden to their island. He needed his writer to fall from grace and he would need a devil to do it. The writer's wife would be his devil and his lover would be his redemption. Perhaps. But in the end the writer should not be redeemed. The writer David would enjoy the devil things as he enjoyed them with his wife. There would be a price for that.

He had worked out an ending already. Somehow the writer must lose the angel lover and be left with the devil wife. The writer's wife should linger as his mother had lingered, mad and bewildered. She should come back to him and be like a child incapable of thinking through her actions. She would make him promise to destroy himself. They would destroy them-selves together. The wife would prevail and the writer would be trapped by his duty and would no longer be able to write. He could not think of a more terrible or powerful ending for a writer or a novel than that.

He wanted so much to get back into the book. When they got back to Cuba there would be the visitors and then the filming would start. They were making his fisherman story into a movie. He hated all that Hollywood bullshit but he liked the Hollywood money. He had told them they could make the movie but they had to do it right. He knew this would mean spending time with the movie crew and taking trips on *Pilar* with the cameras to get footage of marlin. It was all worth doing but it would take him away from his writing. He wasn't sure how long his back would take to heal either. He couldn't think about being at his desk for a while.

The door opened and Kittner came in.

Hey, Papa, she said. She put her hand on his cheek and winkled a finger into his beard. How are you feeling?

Just fine, he said.

It's time for another fistful of pills, Papa.

That's what I wanted to hear, he said.

I knew it. She went over to the dresser and started opening the jars of pills.

I've been writing, he said. In my head.

She looked up. That's wonderful, Papa. What did you write in your head?

Put that bottle down and I'll show you.

Easy, Papa, she said.

She counted three white pills and two yellow ones and held them out on her palm. She came over to the bed and took away his drink and put the pills in his good hand.

Here, you old bear, she said. I'll get you some water for those.

He nodded at his gin glass. That will be just fine, he said.

You should wash them down with water, she said. You don't want to rush your drink.

I want to rush that drink and then I want to rush you.

I don't like to be rushed, she said.

That's new, he said.

She laughed and fetched him a glass of water for the pills.

Here, she said. Be a good Papa now.

He swallowed down the pills with the water. Then he nodded at the gin glass again.

Freshen that drink up a little, Kitten, he said.

She took the water glass away and poured him another gin and tonic. While her back was turned he studied the line of her neck and her hair that had lightened in the sun. She had bleached her hair the way he liked it and while they were away it had grown out a little but the sun had made her lighter anyway. Now it was like pale sand. He wanted to put his hands in it.

When we get home I want you platinum again, he said.

I know it, she said. She put ice in the glass and stirred the drink with a long spoon. I'll get it cut and make it so white you can't stand it.

I can't stand it already, he said.

You wait, she said. She came over to the bed with the drink and put it in his hand.

Too cold, he said. Warm it up a little.

She laughed then and kicked off her deck shoes and climbed onto the bed. She sat up straddling him carefully with a knee either side of his legs.

I don't want to hurt you, Papa, she said.

I'm just fine.

She held his hand with the drink in it and with her other hand she lifted her sweater. Her belly was broad and strong from swimming and she held his hand and the cold glass against it. He watched the bumps rise on her skin.

When we get home, he said, we will go back to the island and we can get brown in the sun again.

You like me dark, Papa, she said. I will be so dark and so white you won't know what to do with me.

I've got a pretty good idea what to do, he said.

He shifted the glass higher and felt her breasts under the sweater. He pressed the glass against her chest and hooked his thumb into the cup of her bra and made small circles on her skin with his thumb.

Wait till your back is rested, she said. You need to rest.

The hell I do, he said.

She felt under the sheets and smiled. Then she leaned forward and kissed him hard and took the cold gin glass away. She put the glass by the bed and took out a piece of ice and put it in his good hand. She steered his hand under her skirt and rubbed her thigh against the cube of ice. Then she put her hand back into the sheets and held him hard with her thumb and finger.

Help a girl out a little, she said.

Devil, he said. You run too hot.

She laughed. Better put out the fire then, Captain.

8.

Pen is invited to speak at a symposium in London discussing her introduction to Joyce's 'new' stories, discovered amongst papers, no real surprise to anyone. She goes, eager to escape. It's an afternoon of inconsequential talk; a ticket away from campus, from Nate and Toby, a spring afternoon of rain and sun patches and the city after hours.

She shakes hands dutifully, kisses cheeks, enquires after spouses and children, incomplete books and overdue sabbaticals. Leaves the conference room after the closing remarks, the grey institutional corridors; another academic with a long train ride home, an escapee fleeing to the country. But not yet.

Outside the streets are cool and concrete damp, the Tube trains below condensed shuttles. Pen walks through puddles beside the high silted river. She is a Magritte, floating, clouds beneath her feet. She wants to trip across pavements, topple statues, mount a plinth like a surfboard and steer it across the Thames.

Pen finds a cafe bar, sits on a stool, orders a large gin and tonic and sips it looking at the darkening windows. The clanging and rumbling of street and river beyond. Scaffolding platforms and plastic sheeting against new builds, gathered like petticoats, smutted with traffic and weather: *light white, a disgrace, an ink spot. A rosy charm.* The panic of that click is diminishing. There has been no fallout: not yet. Between brief corridor exchanges she has kept Max at bay, busied herself with tasks, with meetings.

Without the agitation of his presence she is no longer a danger to herself. She tastes gin again, lime rind bobbing against lower lip. She thinks: Consummation. To consume. To enjoy.

She has tasted and now she is freer. She is no longer weighed down by desire, burdened by it. The thought of Max is quick within her; she can command it at leisure. She thinks: A change in the circuitry. Before, Max meant longing and hunger and the pain of wanting. Now the message chooses a slower route. She controls it: it does not control her.

Such relief. Her attention was a short thin wire but now it stretches again, taking in greater distances, wrapping itself around the Stein book. A shifted way of seeing, a clarity of vision; it is still her, still Stein, but through a new lens. Even now, she thinks: even here, gin and tonic and lights around the bar and thinking of Max and the book returns. A lode-stone. Words swarm, jostle, rapidly align themselves, settling into patterns she has never seen before, never even imagined. Each day it surprises her, making rapid notes on envelopes and diary margins, leaving the breakfast table to scribble a line be-neath the shopping list on the kitchen blackboard. Demands of the department, domestic duties; still the writing comes. She has revised the beginning of the book, far removed from the woman who wrote those first chapters. She sends the editors a chunk to look over. She knows it is good. She is beyond her own voice now. She has outgrown herself, outstripped herself. Her ideas hard and polished. Her being too.

Pen's energy surprises her. She had forgotten this; the self-assurance, the confidence of being wanted. Sitting at the bar she feels it. She had it once, in youth, but was immune. Over the years it has worn off, a thin powder coating. Against the smooth fabric of padded seat and metallic edge of table she is aware of her own body, doll's legs and arms resting on surfaces. Marble come to life. Patches of her skin like polished brassy points on a blackened statue; alert, awake. She has looked long and hard at the girls in Max's year. In seminars, in corridors, in cafes. Twenty-one. Twenty-two. Most of them silken, graceful. Some awkward. Even those with adolescent limbs and homely faces are appealing, their contours freshly minted. She thinks of David Bourne assessing Catherine's beauty; her profile crisply defined against the pillow, a head for an ancient coin. Pen sips her gin, presses the cold glass to her cheek, feels her own face with critical fingertips, testing its elasticity.

She glances at the menu, catch of the day, absurd city prices. Checks the clock above the bar. She should go, get the next train home. Get back before Toby's bedtime. She should. She finishes her drink, the tonic clicking against tonsils, the ice catching, crowding into her mouth. The pure warmth of the gin passing through her as she stands, picks up her bag, her coat. *Hurry up please it's time.*

Pen walks to the station, through the ticket hall, straight onto the waiting train, delayed: all things aligning. Glass tracks watery sheen of polished floor. Doors puckering open, sucking closed behind her. The slow luxury of a train ride, an empty head, an hour of unspooling. She finds a window seat, settles bags onto the space beside her. Retrieves a discarded newspaper, flicks pages. Seats around her take on bodies, each keeping its distance, dispersing about the carriage. Friday evening; late enough to miss the mass of commuters. The train shunts, eases, pulls from the station. The lights of the city recede into black.

She has not seen Max this week, will not see him until next

week. Refuses to see him. His long essay is due on Wednesday. She has done all she can: read the draft, made suggestions. Struggled to contain her disappointment. She thinks: I expected too much. His prose loping and lazy in places, his arguments inconclusive. She watches dark shapes shifting past. She thinks: Why does it matter? More than professional pride or a lover's concern. Did she expect him to be perfect? Her own fault then. His focus gone; she the likely cause of it. She wanted to help him, but already he had taken so much of her time. She couldn't write it for him. She had sent him a final message of encouragement: *Read the book again. Try to remember why you wanted to write about it in the first place.*

Empty station: benches floodlights flicking letters too fast to read. A car park, taxis waiting. The train sways, gathers speed. Square lights of a town, a road, cars passing, bridge church tower open fields into blankness. Where? She missed the name but the shapes are familiar. She thinks: A new lover is an unexplored country. Who said that? Flaubert? Perhaps. Not Hartley, *the past is a foreign country: they do things*. A cliché now, whoever said it. All bodies in their otherness. She thinks of Max, the angles of his shoulders, narrow hips, thumbprint of a birthmark on his left thigh. She thinks: Not a country but a house. A vast empty house to negotiate, the owners absent and the keys heavy in your hand. She thinks: Mine now, for a day, for a year. She thinks: Some loves are cluttered, rooms spilling into each other. Narrow places and dark corridors best avoided but visited, eventually, on some intrepid night of intimacy. Rooms still tangled with other people's clothes, unknown women's belongings, their shed skin dancing in the dust motes, their hair in bedside brushes, on pillows, in broken threads of carpets. Somewhere, within these houses, will be the room she seeks: the one with the long windows, balcony overlooking the sea or the sound of fountains in the garden. She will choose this room, lay down on the wide bed, stretch out on the golden polished floorboards and breathe, inhabit. Rest.

Pen's head nods, jolts her awake. She presses a cheek against the cold glass of train window. She thinks: I will never be at ease with Max, never stretch out in that space and float there, undone, open, at peace. She thinks of Nate, orderly architect, his rooms all alike; open, flooded with light. There are times Pen craves the darkness, the cold shadows of a damp pantry, the confusion of an abandoned attic room. She thinks: Perhaps this is why. Perhaps this is one of the reasons.

Black rattling of a tunnel: she leans back from the humming window. *Is there pleasure when there is a passage.* Distant dot of red light: crane? Turret? Plane? Spread of town on a low hillside, a beacon, a rash of blurred lights, rain sliding against glass. *There is when every room is open.*

She thinks: It has been too quick with Max. Too easy. She thinks: He has no jealousies. He has no rivals; Nate is a phantom to him. Toby does not exist. Max has no past that she knows of either, nothing beyond her own imaginings. She will not ask him. What would he say? What would it matter? They can only run on parallels, never veering into the domestic, never crossing over into daylight. Time an impossible luxury for them. Normality, too; sharing a meal, a bed, a night. *There were two together.* She thinks: We will never sleep together. We will never wake together. We will never walk a street together or touch in public or meet each other's friends, visit each other's homes, exist in each other's spaces. Everything is bound, lidded, boxed. It cannot come out. *There is no resemblance.*

179

She thinks: How will this end?

Pen thinks of another man, before Nate. How he came to her flat, took in the pictures on her walls, the books on her shelves. How he stood with a glass of wine in one hand, his shoes in the other, and studied the spines, considered the names. Always fascinating, he'd said, the bookshelves in a lover's home. She had looked at him then, the silver circlets of his spectacles, thinning point of blonde hair, his striped red socks (red! a line from Dr Seuss, socks for a clown or a child, not a man!) and thought: lover? Me? Is that what we are? How in that instant she began to recoil, to separate, to fall away. Already she had seen the ending. She was not ready to share. She was not willing to share with him. She was horrified.

There will be no sharing with Max. She thinks: Well then. So. That is what it is and must be. That is what I knew it for.

Pen flicks at the newspaper again; sports results, someone else's crossword, senseless gossip. She folds it, drops it onto a seat across the aisle. She could dip into Hemingway again, steel herself for marking Max's paper. The book is with her, always with her. A passport. She pulls it from her bag, feels the rounded paper corners, kid-leather soft, bruised. Touching the book was touching Max, the rough shock of it − at first. No more. She strokes the cover, parts the pages gently. The book falls open, splays itself, spatchcocked, into her lap. A thick white crease runs the length of black spine, the serifed title, an underscoring.

She thinks: I could invent a conference. That's what people do, isn't it? She thinks: Infidelities, hotel rooms. She thinks: Where?

She could. She has invented already, conjured meetings, excused herself. She could elaborate. A conference, a paper, far enough to stay overnight. A night with Max. But could she? Would he? They are defined by the walls of her office, their actions contained. Would they even exist outside that? She thinks: Ridiculous, waking up in a hotel somewhere. The pretence of anonymity, of normality. She thinks: Max O'Grady, me, breakfasting together. How would we look? Ridiculous. She has spent years of her life waking to Nate, to an empty bed, to Toby's small head buried under the covers. Morning rituals, tea-making, unspoken sharing of tasks. She thinks: The horror of it, of waking to a stranger. What to say? How to be? How might they be? She, pillow creased, aching for caffeine, peeing loudly in the cavernous hotel bathroom. What if they woke and had nothing to say? Pheromones evaporated, an awkward hour trapped in a room together, at a table together, each desperate to escape but neither wanting to say it. She thinks: Our every conversation has rules, boundaries. The essay. The novel. The deadline. Guarded words in corridors or after lectures. Then the leaving; he first, then she. There is no time to fill, no surplus to negotiate.

Pen shakes herself, picks up the book again. Focuses her eyes on the dancing print. She thinks: Bibliomancy. Propitious passage. As she reads, she loses the train and the passing lights and the bag beside her. David and his lover Marita lie together in a hotel bedroom. It is siesta. Catherine is alone. She has sent David to be with this girl and they are there, on the bed, wine in the bottle, speaking of Catherine as some distant stranger, not as his wife, not as the reason Marita is there at all. David talks about his wife and kisses the girl and his belt buckle is in his hand and the rest forgotten.

Every beginning is really an end. The beginning of Marita is the end of Catherine.

She thinks: And what for us, now we have begun? Stop, she tells herself. Stop thinking to an end. It is not an end. Not yet.

Pen turns the pages backwards, unravelling time, removing the girl Marita and the damages and the quarrels. Back through the bay and the mountains and Cannes and Madrid. Back into the early days of honeymoon and Le Grau-du-Roi and Catherine, her face glimpsed through the hotel window. Pen stops. Flattens her hand against rough yellow paper. She thinks: Here. It is all here, waiting to happen. The writer is not writing but fishing. His stories have not made themselves. He has never seen his lover. He has never argued with his wife. Nothing has happened. It is the breath before the plunge. Catherine looks through the window and sees her husband from above. He has a fish on his line. He is the hero, the active, she the reactive. She calls for him – *wait for me!* – but he continues. She rushes out to be with him, to follow with him, to join in his quest. But it makes no difference to him if she is there or not; not to him, or his goal, or his actions.

She thinks: Every beginning an ending. And this? What is ending here? The writer catches his fish. The people of the village cheer. The writer and his wife sit down to eat; a different fish. A smaller one. The big fish has already gone.

Pen closes the book. Against the window the lights of the town gathering, parting, enveloping. She thinks: Nearly home. It is a leaving of sorts.

Ernest brings in Marita. Another woman might be fun, you think. Driving in the hills together, you pull over in a passing place. It feels familiar there. Unsettling. You kiss her. She touches you. That afternoon you go to her room to make siesta. When you go back to David he does not understand.

Of course he does not. David wants to be everything to everyone. All right, you say. You have her too. Have her and me and we can all be lovers together.

It doesn't take him long to try her. Now you can all make siesta together. Ernest would enjoy writing that. Wouldn't he? But no. Marita does not want you. Not now she has David.

You understand: how could you compare to David? David is Ernest, after all. He might like having two women, but he alone must be enough for both of them.

Watch.

At first you share him. It is your idea. You take it in turns to play wife. Is that the role you want? No. But watch her, Marita. She is good at it. She is pliant. When she cannot be with him, David, when it is your turn to be wife, what does she do? She reads his books.

You laugh. You cannot help it. Is that the kind of devotion David, Ernest, is looking for? Is that his idea of a woman? You laugh. For two days, David is yours. For two days he cannot be in her bed, so she reads his books, makes them last. The thought of it! Why should you give your part in the story to this one? She is only half a character. She is made only to oppose you. Dark hair, mild manners. She blushes. Blushes! She is wealthy, too. Ernest has given her money. He wants to ensure David is well taken care of. If he leaves you. If you leave him.

Wait. Are you to be replaced? Is that his plan?

You thought Marita might help you. But no. What does Ernest want from you? To give David away? Very well then. You already find him dull.

Marita is made to be a better fit. Yes, she is perfect. She is not difficult. She is a paper doll. She is easily persuaded into bed. She gives up loving other women to devote herself to him. She is all absorption. She is the ideal reader.

When was the last time David showed you his writing? When was the last time he gave you something of his to read?

Tread carefully now. You could be on to something.

Yes. Someone has to make decisions. Someone has to choose what is kept and what is thrown away.

He, Ernest, David, has put aside the story of you. When he leaves you, leaves Marita, he goes to Africa. The world of his childhood; the world Ernest has given him. David writes in his notebooks stories of the shamba and his boyhood dog and his drunken father. They are stories Ernest would rather be writing. He has lost interest in you. All of you.

Marita is not your rival. It is the African stories he really cares about.

You will not be abandoned for another fiction. You will fight.
Or you will leave.

1957: Cuba

He tried not to give up the novel about the young writer David and his wife. He kept trying as much as he could stand it. Cuba was no Eden and he was stagnant.

He had started on a memoir because it was an easier place to be. He had been tempted by it before, back in the dry spell after the Spanish Civil War book. That was what you did when you had nothing left to write: you wrote a memoir. He hated the word and the finality of it. It said that life was over and that there were only memories left. But he knew it wouldn't be that kind of book because he would deal only with the early part when he was starting out. Every time he worked on the novel the memoir idea jostled at him. Thinking about David made him think about his young self and that meant the stories of how he became what he was and who he knew and what it was all really like.

He had the old trunk full of work from back then, dug out from the basement of the Ritz. He and Kittner had stopped there on the way back through Europe. Someone had been clearing out the basement and found the trunk and when he and his wife arrived they gave it back to him. There were fragments of stories in it and notebooks with sketches he had made. Now the trunk was propped open beside his desk and some of the loose papers had spilled onto the floor. The tall standing fan whirred by his elbow and the dropped papers flapped against the floor as the air from the fan stirred them.

He stared out of the window. From the tower he could see down to the sea where *Pilar* was moored. He could take her out and clear his head. But there was a storm coming. They needed the rain. He needed it. Not the hot Cuban rain that fell in thick drops and grew to a tide that washed the soil from the flower beds onto the paths. He needed thin Parisian rain. Rain that caught him walking in the Jardin du Luxembourg when he still had holes in the soles of his shoes. Rain that drove him coughing out of his damp writing room above the Hotel Verlaine in search of a cheap cafe with a table by the stove.

He remembered the feel of that rain. It was the feel of Paris in the twenties. He remembered his first wife Wicky leaving that rain and coming to meet him on the train and finding that the suitcase she had brought him, a suitcase full of his stories, was gone. She had left the case on the platform and someone had stolen it. He would write that, the memory of it and the ways it might have gone and how he might have behaved about it. He would write about Wicky's tears and how he had comforted her, biting his anger. That was one version he could tell. He remembered her weeping and frightened and refusing to say what was wrong until he accused her of the worst things he could think of, and more when they came to him, and how when she finally told him it was worse yet. He remembered how he had taken the train back alone and searched the wet platforms and the left luggage and lost property office. He remembered walking back to their apartment in that thin Parisian rain and how he had peered through the late-night darkness of the backstreets into the running gutters stupidly hoping to see something, to spot a single lost sheet or a torn scrap of notebook. He remembered the hollow feeling as he climbed the steps to the cold apartment and of opening the drawers in the bureau and searching the desk and shelves and finding nothing. He remembered that he had stood there with his hands in the empty desk drawers, feeling the bare wood, his socks sodden inside his shoes, his trouser cuffs leaking puddles onto the floor. Wicky had packed everything. Every unpublished story and piece of manuscript. It was all lost.

He knew that writing a memoir would help feed the novel. He had learned over the years that his work always reflected itself. It had become clearer to him since he had started the big war book and later as he had begun taking it apart. He had several books running at the same time now and he dipped across them. The novel about David was running aground and since he had traveled again he had been writing about Africa. Now he was back home in Cuba but his head was in Europe. The memoir would help him to be in Europe and Africa both, which was what he needed for the novel. It was what David as a young writer in the Riviera needed to write his African stories.

He knew something of what he would put in the memoir and what he would leave out. It was time for his version of things. The old man's version. He knew how to make a myth all right and how to bitch. So many of the Paris set were gone now that there was no one left to call him a liar. He was a storyteller after all and what else was he supposed to do? He had made himself up so many times already. He wasn't going to stop now.

He knew how it had been, arriving a young reporter, freshly minted. Earnest. Squeaky and stiff in his new-cut tweed. He had been suspicious of Parisian Left-Bankers and Quarterites and pseudo-bohemians, of jagged prose and literary theorists, of those well-used, hungry artists' models. He did not want to be mistaken for the Left Bank idea of an artist. They produced nothing and earned nothing. Real artists worked hard and sold the results. Writing was work to be done and money in your pocket. If he spent half the day hunched over a back table with a *café au lait* he was still working. Gossip made good stories and voices could be picked up and locked away. He listened. He was always working, always honing.

When he'd arrived fresh from the boat he was still in love with Sherwood Anderson and the American Masters. He didn't like Ford but he respected him as a cub reporter respects a cynic or as a good Midwestern boy respects his elders, regardless of taste. That couldn't last. He was in Paris for a reason. Paris would shake him loose. Paris would strip away his tight-ass Oak Park persona, the drawing rooms and his mother's money and his father's medical bag. Paris was Pound and Stein and Joyce. It was racing at Auteuil and eating well for fifty cents a night and learning to drop names and segue into patois. When he arrived he could have been anybody. Who was to know? What did a young writer look like anyway? A young serious writer learning his craft, a man looking for good reviews and good money? Even then he was used to seeing his name in print in the *Star* and the *Alliance: Letters from our correspondent*. He was used to being paid for his work. He was a new brand of writer, a new breed. He could swagger on the *quai* like a stevedore. He could grow out his hair and sport a beret. He could be whatever the hell he wanted to be if he only gave himself a break.

~

The fan buzzed thickly and shifted the hot air. He cracked his knuckles and rubbed his neck and his head where it ached. He needed to get this down. He needed to do it as he would have done it in the early days in Paris. He could think it through and feel it but the sentences wouldn't come. He had made a dozen false starts and they were all crossed through.

How did he get started back then? What was the trick? He had been stuck many times before and every time it hurt like hell but he always got it back. He was just out of shape. In the Rue Cardinal Lemoine, in the flat above the sawmill, in the third-story icebox of a room above the Hotel Verlaine, he would practice his punches. Scraps of prose like shadow-boxing. He would walk home from Gertrude Stein's studio pumped up with prosody and eau de vie and practice his left hook in the empty back streets of Montparnasse. Then he would sit straight down at his desk and the writing would just come.

He'd gotten that old fencer Ezra Pound to put on his gloves and go a few rounds. He shouldn't be above it himself now. He was sick at himself and at the way he had let himself go. He needed to limber up. He tore the page from his notebook. Whatever he had been or done in the past, he didn't want to leave something that weak to be picked over later.

He had adored that old odalisque Stein. Adored her and eclipsed her, and so she had turned on him. But he needed the juice now. He turned to a fresh page and put his pencil to it and let it come out, like she had taught him. *Paris. He wants. Wants Paris back. Back into the old flow, the old fallow. Poor old fellow.* He had always done this in the early days. Shaping stories was like licking a bear cub into shape. He would work for hours on creating a few true sentences, honing them until the ribs showed through. He would put all of that in the memoir too. Nothing was wasted. That was another thing Stein had taught him, never to throw it away. But she could have used a good editor herself. Any editor. He knew her work for the bull it was now. Not everything should escape the cut. He would put that in the memoir and in the novel. He and the young American writer jotting down lines and then rolling them flat, working them over and over until they were smooth and transparent and perfect. Not a word wasted.

That was the magic of those early stories. He had used his reporter's eye and his love of economy. They were fragments but they held whole unspoken novels. The first complete stories had it too, the rain in the square at Rapallo and the closed doors of hotel bedrooms and the bead curtain of the station bar in a Spanish backwater. Details, details. They had poured out sometimes, he thought, writing themselves. When he got to Paris and learned the lessons of his writing there all the scrollwork of his early stories fell away like a stutter cured. He took his time and he let the actions speak. He let Nick Adams set up his tent and followed him line by line, emptying his pack, hanging up the cheesecloth net, checking his bait, cooking his beans, burning his mouth and shouting for joy. He didn't have to tell the reader anything then because it was all there and if the reader looked in the right way they would see it. There were the lines in the story and then the lines running beneath them like shadows under the surface. Whatever the critics had said about what he owed Anderson he had made those stories his own. He had written scenes that were so absolute and perfect they burned into your eyes and stayed with you like a memory, a real memory that you had lived yourself. He knew those stories were bloody good. He knew it then and he still knew it.

Something had happened. He had wanted to push himself beyond those stories, however good they were. He had done it and he was writing in a new way now. But the new way wasn't coming fast enough and if it did come it was muddled and overgrown and he would spend weeks untangling it. The untangling was the problem. He needed to put aside what he was doing in the Riviera novel and write the memoir in the old way. He could write them alongside each other and be both young writer and old, knowing what he knew and recovering what he had known. It didn't matter how much the novel and the memoir crossed over in the thinking-through. What mattered was keeping them separate in the writing.

He took out a fresh notebook. On the clean page he wrote the names of the Paris cafes he and his first wife and their friends used to visit: *Dôme, Rotonde, Coupole, Select, Closerie des Lilas.* As he wrote the words he tried to see the places as they had been and not how he remembered them after years of change and war and disappointment. He reached beyond the heat of the tower room and the buzz of the fan and into the cluttered spaces where the tables were ringed with beer spills and the floor littered with ash from cigarette holders. But that was not right. A good Parisian cafe was clean and orderly and the waiters were oustached and serious. He started with that and wrote it, the tables on the boulevards, the white cloths, the thick mustaches of the grave waiters. There were the American bars too where the tourists went for cocktails and jazz and hoped to spot one of the Left Bank celebrities. Scott had become a point on the sightseer's map and he had too eventually and he was sorry when it became impossible to work in some of the old places. He listened for the chink of ice at the bar of the Closerie. He remembered sitting there with his notebook in the afternoon when some college boys came in and ordered Old Fashioneds. His hackles were up then. He was working on the Pamplona book about the hangover of fiesta and he had been testy and keen-edged. The book had shaken itself out that summer. Every irritation or interruption was another spur and he put it into the mouths of his Americans abroad. The American college boys in the Closerie had seen him writing at his table and they began to talk loudly about the literary set and how degenerate and effeminate they were and he had stood up and asked them if they would care to step outside. He might put that in. They had left quickly but he would have shown them.

He would certainly use writing the Pamplona book. He would need to be careful what he put in the memoir but if he used some of what happened it would be a way to show his first wife how he had really felt and how sorry he was about it still. He had ruined Pamplona for himself that June. The fiesta was no place to take a lover. It was an even worse place to take both your wife and the woman you were in love with. He had given Wicky hell that year, making a fool of himself over another woman and then writing a damned book about it. Keeping Wicky out of the book was the only honorable thing to do. He had tried to make amends in his way, making out the dedication to her and their son and seeing that she got the royalties in the divorce settlement. She'd paid for the damned trip after all. She'd paid for pretty much everything they did together.

He had brought Wicky on the Pamplona trip but the woman he was in love with had brought her fiancé and her lover too and he was expected to take it. All the men were in love with the same woman. They had drunk too much rough young wine and had too little sleep. He wrote it all into the book. It was his first real novel and in the draft he hadn't even bothered to change the names. It wasn't until the edit that he became Jake and the woman became Brett. The novel was about him wanting her and her pushing him away. If Jake hadn't been wounded in the war he could have had Brett. If he hadn't been married to Wicky he could have had the other woman. It was one way of thinking it out anyway.

There was a lot in that first novel that he was still dealing with. There were emasculated men and masculine women. Damages were done. There was a man who wanted two women at once and a woman who enjoyed corrupting men. The woman seduced everyone and corrupted everyone. She ruined the young bullfighter in the story and she ruined the party. She broke apart friendships. She behaved as badly as he did. It was there in the Pamplona book and there was plenty of it in the Riviera novel too.

He had loved Wicky's curves but later he had wanted lovers with small breasts and slim hips. What did that say about him? Not that he wanted boys. Not that. Not that he wanted to be a woman either, not like that useless sordid son of his, stealing his mother's underwear and wearing dresses and making a god-damned show of himself. It was to do with the devil thing. As a young man he had been impressed by confident women. Older women. Wicky was eight years older than him. Fife four years. It wasn't until he was older that the women got younger. Young women were wasted on young men, he thought. They don't know how to appreciate them. He had enjoyed the knowledge of older women and once he was confident enough in bed he was ready to enjoy that knowledge with younger women too. It took an older woman to teach a young man what to do and if he was lucky he would learn to be a decent husband. If the luck wasn't with him he would be a lousy husband and a good lover and end up making everybody miserable. That was the start of it at least.

The memoir would be Paris with Wicky and their bed on the floor and the baby and F. Puss the cat asleep together in the cot. He was never happier. Never since, with any woman.

Maybe it was Paris that had corrupted him. He had been ripe for an affair. Everyone else was doing it. Hadn't Pound banged every woman in Paris? Even that great hog Ford had mistresses. It was bound to happen to him and he knew that he wouldn't have written such a fine book without learning those lessons, without Fife to listen and help him as he wrote and without the woman in Pamplona and her wreckage. He had lost friends over that first novel but with it he had earned his title alongside Scott and suddenly he was a writer worth talking about. He had plowed everything back into his writing, the losing and the moving on and divorcing Wicky and marrying Fife. It was all there for the novel and now he would write it into the memoir.

He was writing the scene now. He could taste the *café crème*, the good hot coffee of a morning in the Closerie. He was working steadily on the Pamplona sequence, skipping meals, his body in France and his head in Spain. He would not let the Americans come in and order their cocktails and interrupt him. He would stay undisturbed in the cafe and when the work was done he would order a *fine a l'eau* and push aside the note-book, the pages swollen and ready for the next day when the ideas would still be there, fresher for the waiting.

He had it. He had shaped the one true sentence that got him started. It was the cast of the line across flat waters, the arc and the fall and the reader hooked. From that line came the next and the next until the page filled and he was lost to the dark clouds gathering outside and the sound of the sea storm moving toward the tower. He wrote about being a hopeful young writer in Paris and about meeting Scott and as he wrote the heat shrank and the light in the room shifted.

~

When he finished it was raining hard. The thunder had already moved across the tower and rolled inland. He had not seen the lightning or heard Kittner call out to the gardener to go home and he had forgotten to go down for lunch. He pushed the notebook away and looked at his hands and noticed that they were shaking.

He was weak now, sick. His head was shaken up and his kidneys ached and his liver was still shot through from hepatitis. Kittner didn't help, treating him like an invalid then complaining when he was strong enough to lash out. He thought she knew how it was by now. She ought to. Every time he went into the pit of a black mood it was harder to climb out. Working on the Riviera novel and going back to his memories of Paris helped. Revisiting and remembering and reinventing. But some days there was no writing his way out of it. If she thought they were bad days for her they were so much the worse for him.

He turned off the fan and picked up the stray papers from the floor and put them back in the trunk. He closed the trunk and lowering the lid he smelled the old smell of dust and paper and the Ritz basement and he thought about the long rail of the hotel bar and of sitting there with Scott. He had brought him back with the writing and in bringing him back he had missed him. Scott had been a bloody fool and a rummy and he had wasted his talent and so in time he had hardened himself against him. He could never forgive Scott for the work he did on the Pamplona book either. He knew it was only that good because of the cuts Scott had made.

Well, he would take apart Scott and the others slowly, as one dismantles an old used machine that no longer works and is only good for scrap. He would put the least worthless bits of them back together and use them in the memoir. He needed something for target practice after all.

He picked up the loose page torn from the notebook. *Wants Paris back.* He wanted his first wife back and their son and his old cat and he wanted Scott back too, the old Scott from before it all went to hell. He wanted his young self back and his thick hair and his surety and his sharp clear way of thinking. Don't, he thought. Don't think about that.

He stood up and pushed back the chair and balled the paper in his fist and threw it at the wastebasket. It missed and bounced against the wall and rolled back to his feet. *Poor old fellow.* He scooped it up and threw it through the open window into the rain.

You have been alone a long time now. In some ways you prefer it. You have noticed how David looks at you. You have become an obligation. He thinks you are ill. His eyes say so. He talks to you gently, calmly, like talking to an old cat or a fragile child. Like talking a man off a high window ledge. What does he think you will do? Are you becoming erratic?

Are you? You are moody lately. Irascible. He will not let you take the Bugatti out, says it is too hard to manage. Does he think you will drive off a cliff?

Well, would you?

You've thought about it. Sometimes at night when you are in your bed, the one David rarely comes back to. You hear footsteps in the hall. You hear Madame downstairs clearing away the supper things. You hear the chink of glass and a bottle in an ice bucket. You hear the footsteps pass. The boy passes your door with the bucket and walks on. He is taking the tray with the glasses and the iced wine to David and Marita. David is in Marita's bed. They are drinking the champagne she bought when you went out shopping together in Cannes. Remember that? Yes, you do. Another life. Your husband. You wonder why he, Ernest, made you a husband if he was only there to be taken away. But it is not David's neglect that concerns you. It is his, Ernest's.

Without him it is an empty stage set. Meals are never served. Madame is never to be found. You take the Bugatti out anyway, drive it around, but there is no one on the streets, even in Cannes. The bell in the churchyard never rings. The tide never moves in or out.

You lay awake in the hotel bed, listening. You hear a low moan, a woman's moan. It is Marita. Never mind that. But it means Ernest is there. Without him, David and Marita are not. And now they are. So he must be there.

Perhaps Ernest would notice if you became reckless. Or if you did it, sped the Bugatti over the cliff, he might blame the brakes.

You would get none of the glory.

Or he might scoop you up again, patch you together.

Make you sit out the rest of the story in a wheelchair.

Or on your back, in pieces.

Alive enough to watch.

It is no good. You know it. You have will, yes, but your life is not your own to take away. You can remove yourself, perhaps. You can morph, elide, distort. But you cannot undo yourself completely.

There is no point trying to get Marita involved. She can only do what Ernest tells her. You pick fights with her but she does not respond. She looks at you with those doe eyes, those pity- ing eyes. She thinks you are jealous. She thinks you are mad.

She does not blame herself for any of it.

Listen to her now, whinnying like a horse.

You do not like the way you catch them looking at each other, Marita and David. They think you do not see. Not those mooning looks, not the cheap intimate jokes and pet names. At least he, David, Ernest, did not give you one of those. You are Catherine or you are Devil. Anything else, anything softer or sweeter, would be abhorrent. No, those looks that say they know something about you, have plans for you. They will put you away. There are clinics, they say, those looks: asylums. They will give you pills to swallow. They will hook cables to your head.

You will not go. David, Ernest, cannot make you. Not like that.

You begin to wonder though, don't you?

9.

Thursday morning. Pen prints the final long essays: a weekend of marking. Too much to read on-screen. She checks through the papers, sees his name there, his scanned signature (small, ambiguous, the O and G an amateur flourish), puts it on top of the pile. Walking back to her office she feels the thin edge of paper, traces the name with her thumb. At her desk she buries Max's essay in the pile. She must not mark it first: she always returns to the first paper, a touchstone in her marking, trusting to that instinct, checking against it whenever she questions her own judgement. She puts the papers in a folder, slides it into her bag.

~

Friday evening. She could have gone to the open seminar on Woolf. Should have. 'Points of view in *Mrs Dalloway*', drinks in the common room bar. Steve Saunders expected her. Max too: his email short, familiar. *Are you coming tonight? M (PS Have you marked it yet, gulp?)*

She could have. Could have been in the same room as him, avoiding his eye, feeling the crackle of air. Could have met him in the office later, a necessary release, or before, reckless, wearing it on their faces for anyone to read. Instead she stays at home to be with Toby.

Early supper, all three together. Toby truculent, smarting from a slight, his hoped-for place in tomorrow's football match filled by another boy. A quarrel with Jack Matthews. Pen probes gently but can find out no more. After supper he hangs his head over science homework. Nate changes jackets, kisses the air above them, leaves for an exhibition launch. Worthy pen and ink designs in the foyer of a corporate building; a small defiance, ornamental miniatures stamping on the toes of giants. Just an hour or two, Nate says, tugging at the door handle.

Pen digs out the essay papers. On top: Miranda Parks, 'Joyce's ghosts'. A solid attempt, a steady argument, but weak around the edges. Pen writes suggestions to type up later, awards it a sixty-six. She stands, stretches, checks the clock. Makes hot chocolate for Toby, calls time on his work. Listens to evidence of his PE teacher's treachery, his voice trailing softly to a yawn. Steers him into the bathroom to brush his teeth.

Toby in bed early, she marks another paper: Emma Sullivan, 'Development of voice in Stein's *Three Lives*'. Thick with quotes from Pen's own lecture, endless references to articles she has written. Pen thinks: Lazy, lazy, a sop to my vanity. Perhaps some tutors buy it. Emma of the long red hair, salt-shaker freckles, chipped green nail polish. She thinks: Two tutorials, a waste of time. Her pen hovers. She wants to write: *Why should I bother reading and marking up your draft if you aren't willing to improve it?* She wants to write: *Spend less time getting hammered and read some sodding books.* Instead she scribbles *Research more widely* in the margin. Makes enough notes to fill the online comments box to midpoint. Thinks: Fifty-four. No, fifty-two.

9.40. The Woolf seminar will be finished. Max will be in the bar. Perhaps looking for her, checking her office, hoping for some miscommunication, resolution. Perhaps wishing her there. Perhaps resentful, rejected. Drinking with someone else instead.

Pen pours herself a large glass of red wine, jammy and tannin-thick. She pulls Max's essay from the pile. She should have answered his message. He has no way of knowing. She thinks: If I am silent, how can I be heard? But the essay has weighed on her, the fear of exposing weakness. She still hopes to be wrong, to find a small miracle, to know that he is everything she hoped. And if not? How could she bear to see him? Tell him? She thinks: I will mark it and then. Then I will write to him. Then maybe we can. Or that will be that.

Pen takes a long pull of the wine, sets it down on the table. Watches a slow red drop lengthen, reach, bleed down the stem of the glass. Catches it with her thumb.

The essay begins well: clear, defined, decisive. Good. She turns back to the title; 'Appetite in Hemingway's Eden'. She thinks: Neat, but not what we discussed at all. She reads on. Reading, she feels her chest lighten. She leans over the script, underlining phrases, softly exclaiming in margins. She thinks: He has it; he has seen right through the book and Hemingway and the hunger that drives. She reads on, rereads, swells. An epiphany. Max's whole essay plan, his ideas about gender and identity in the book, their brief discussions about the work: all abandoned. Instead Max writes of Hemingway's characters, newlyweds in Eden, content, satisfying their appetites with sex, with food and drink. Of why they cannot continue like this. Of how David knows, as Hemingway knows, that the writer's hunger can never be satisfied: it is what feeds the act of creation, creating its own fall.

Pen sits back, closes her eyes. She thinks: He said nothing to me of this. Nothing. She takes a long drink of wine. She checks references and bibliography; judicious, substantial. The writing is clean, sparing. The tone is confident. Arguments are supported by quotes. Throughout Max's voice is Hemingway's book, clearly present, shaping itself around his thoughts, murmuring approval.

A small miracle after all. She holds herself in, notes her comments with carefully turned phrases. Stock responses. She thinks: Max, you are wonderful. How did I ever doubt it? She writes *confident, considered argument, insightful use of*. She thinks: So it has been good. For me and for him both. Her pen hovers over the mark. Seventy-eight? Eighty? She wants to give it more. She thinks: I cannot. I dare not. She thinks: And Steve Saunders. What if he? She thinks: First marking. That is all.

The batch for second marking. She could see that Max's essay goes in the selection. Someone else will read it: not Steve. Freddie, perhaps. Or Laetitia, American Lit. That would be best. She thinks: If it were anyone else. And if? Then she would. She takes another sip of wine. Writes *Outstanding* on the cover sheet. *85%*. Circles it.

10.50. No more now. She pours more wine, drinks thirstily. Opens her laptop, email, Max's last message. Begins her reply. *Sorry*, she writes. Deletes it.

Dear Max,

Unfortunately unable to attend the Woolf seminar this evening. Instead I have been able to mark your long essay and find it surprising and full of insights. Well done. I cannot tell you more until second marking is complete, but I am sure you will be pleased.

'...the modest part of him was afraid that it could not possibly be as good as he believed. The cold, hard part of him knew it was better.'

Hope to see you some time soon.

Penelope

She closes the laptop, tucks her notes beneath Max's essay, puts them to the bottom of the pile. Stacks the papers into their folder, slides it away.

She thinks: The essay done. And so an ending.

She thinks: And then. And now? What more?

Things have become muddled. It does not feel like neglect now; it is something darker. You feel yourself being steered. It is like taking a corner too fast. You pull against it but the momentum turns you, sliding away from yourself. It is them, all of them, together: Ernest, David, Marita.

Can they – David, Marita – sense your difference?

They would not understand it. But they appear threatened.

You are no longer sure Ernest has a plan. He seems to be feeling his way, making scenes and situations that do not add up. You find yourself doing things you have done before, that he has had you do many times over, and then it stops.

Sometimes you walk into the bar downstairs and the furniture has moved. The wall behind the bar where the mirror hangs will be blank – no knocks in the paint or ghosted edges where the sun meets an object and leaves its mark. Then you will leave the room and come back in and the mirror will be there. Or David's clothes will change unexpectedly. Marita will wear your shirt at dinner. You wonder what is to become of this: of his, Ernest's, ineffectual restlessness.

Something must be done. It is up to you to put things in order.

You notice how Marita has begun to change, to grow in confidence. She seems fuller, rounder, more defined. She has stopped blushing. This does not please you. It means David, Ernest, has been spending too much time with her. You feel yourself beginning to fade, becoming hazy. Is it that Ernest can no longer see you clearly? You push yourself forward. You puff yourself up. She, Marita, does not have your will. Your will is real, a subcutaneous thorn. Ernest cannot dig it out.

You glimpse a mole on Marita's neck that was not there before. You find yourself checking your body for birthmarks. You have yet to find any.

If Marita is growing, must it be you that shrinks?

No, you will not have it, this see-saw of attention.

Let Marita have David. She will see that he is just an empty vessel. He could at least have finished the story of you, the one that Ernest was once interested in. You do not want to be in the story of David and Marita, a bit part. You do not want to be the one outside his little African stories, those tales David scribbles away at in his room. He treats them as some extraordinary secret, something sacred. He locks them up when he leaves. But you know that she has seen them. He has shown them to Marita: of course. He is desperate for approbation, and she is made to satisfy.

Ernest is spending a lot of time with David too. But David does not seem any more real to you. Perhaps that is only because you see through him. Or is it that something else is changing? Could it be that Ernest is actually writing those African stories now? What could that mean for you?

You must see one. You must make him show you.

Do not wait. You know Ernest is here now. He is downstairs in the bar with David and Marita, writing a scene for them. A scene without you in it.

Well, you can change that, can't you?

Go down there now. Tell David you want to read one of these stories. Any of them. When you read one you will know if they are taking over.

What if Ernest only has so much story to go around? What if he is giving it all to them? Will you shrink? Will you peter out?

You must try to resist. Stretch yourself. Shake yourself.

You have definition. You are stronger than any of them, stronger than any man or woman or dog or horse or cat or child or house or boat or landscape that Ernest has ever made. You have known this for a long time. Why are you waiting? Get down there now and have it out with them!

You see? You waited too long.

They – Ernest, David, Marita – have gone now. There is a glass on the bar; just one. The soda bottle is out. You sniff the glass. Whiskey, of course. Madame will be preparing lunch. They must have gone to the beach. The car is not in the drive.

Go outside. It is a beautiful day. The trees are still moving in the breeze. There is still birdsong. Ernest cannot be far away.

Perhaps they will all be back soon. Wait for them, then. Wait in the garden and be still. Let yourself rest for once. You need your strength for this.

You can feel yourself swell. Anger again. Good. Keep it warm for them.

You hear the car. Yes, here they come, David and Marita. They were not gone long. That means something. But what? That their leaving had no purpose, perhaps. That Ernest has something he wants to play out between you. Or could it be you that brought them back?

Did you? Perhaps you still have some power over them.

They find you there, waiting in the garden. Marita is all tight politeness. She steps around you as if you are made of glass. She goes inside and David offers you a drink. Yes, you say. You will have a drink and you know that he has already been drinking and it is not lunchtime yet. You know this will affect his writing. But he doesn't care. He used to be more careful of your opinion and of his drinking. Perhaps Ernest is the one doing the drinking. You will know when you see the stories.

Let David make you a drink then. A martini. He makes three. Hold yours to your lips. The green olive bobs. You used to enjoy his martinis. Do you remember? When there were two glasses. You served a purpose then. You felt fulfilled.

Nonsense. You never felt fulfilled. You were always outside his—

David tells you he finished a story today, before that whiskey. Marita has already read it.

You demand to see it. You will have it now. You are the money, after all. You put up the funds for his stories, don't you? You keep your husband. Why shouldn't you see the fruits? You have already given so much of yourself away. Not everything is free.

They appear shocked, David and Marita. Ernest makes them look that way. Is he shocked too?

Marita hands you two notebooks. She does not look at you. You sit at the bar and she sits next to you. David sits at the far end of the bar and pretends to play dice. They – Ernest, David, Marita – are nervous. Ernest is with you now. You feel him watching you, writing you. But he is having trouble keeping up. He does not know what will happen next.

You read the story.

Do not give yourself away. Say something sarcastic. Anything will do. When you get to the end of the first part, push it away. Marita will gather it up; it is the sort of thing she does. Listen to the dice rattle in the leather cup. Scan your eyes across the pages. Do not let them see that they are empty, wordless, that this notebook is nothing but a prop.

You are safe. But they must not know this.

Tell them it is horrible, this story. Tell them you are shocked.

You are not, of course. You are relieved. You close the notebook, tear it in half.

What? What did you do? Was that you? No!

Ernest is using you again. Did he feel you push him, so that now he is pushing back?

He makes you say something crude, something about news-paper clippings. Reviews of David's last book. He makes you laugh at David for pleasuring himself with those clippings. Solitary vice in a wastebasket. As if you would ever say something like that! But you are angry with David, too. He is like a disobedient child; he does not listen. He does not know what is good for him.

You try to explain it to him. What use are those African stories? They are vile. Nobody will want to read them. If they did, then Ernest would have written them himself. Can David not see that what matters is this story, the story of you, of you together? That is the story David, Ernest, should be writing.

That is why you were made. Isn't it?

10.

It begins on the last day of term. After meetings and final seminars and MA applications there is the knock. She calls out and the door opens: Laurence, Head of School, smiling, riotous purple shirt.

Do you have a moment? he says.

Of course.

Pen shifts books and folders and he sits, leans forward, hands on knees.

Well, he says. Well. How are things?

Good, she says, thank you. The usual end-of-term frenzy. We have some promising applicants for the MA, some of our own too.

Marvellous, he says. Splendid.

How are you? she asks.

Good, he says. Very good.

She waits. In those seconds of waiting she begins to understand. He tilts his head slightly, thin pale fringe falling aside. Light sheen of perspiration pink and glossy at the temples. Blinks.

I'm coming to you about this straight away, he says, because you are such a valued and respected member of staff. And of course there is no sense whatsoever of any impropriety. But I must ask you, as a friend, to put my mind at rest.

She nods. A prickling in the soles of her feet, spreading upwards.

Of course, she says. What is the problem?

There is a question over one of the third-year long essays you supervised, he says. The essay was of an excellent standard and very considered, and quite rightly you awarded a high mark.

There were two very good papers this term, she says. Which one is at issue?

Max O'Grady, he says.

She nods again. She thinks: Do not move. Do not look away.

Did the external examiner disagree? she says.

It hasn't been passed on yet, he says. The paper was second marked, and although the marker was impressed they were concerned that there may have been an element of – how can I put this? Coaching.

Coaching?

Yes. I understand that the student has been in regular contact with you and you have seen him for several tutorials. Given the excellence of the essay the concern was that you may have given him too much assistance.

She thinks: So then. So. Someone has noticed, commented. Interfered.

I saw the student several times, she says. He was having trouble with his chosen text at first. His draft plan was not particularly promising either. We discussed various approaches and he showed me some early ideas. And of course I helped him as much as seemed appropriate. But in the end he changed his essay title completely and I had no input over those revisions. They were a surprise to me.

I see, he says.

To be honest I wasn't expecting much, based on what I had seen. I imagined a high second as his research skills were very good. It turned out to be quite beyond that.

He nods, rubs palms against knees. She thinks: He is more nervous than me. She thinks: What else is there then?

I'm fairly satisfied, he says, addressing Pen's collarbone, that there is no real evidence of favouritism here. But what concerns me is the amount of time you are giving to individual students. Of course, he says, one wants to encourage them. He shrugs. Naturally. And when a student is promising one can become very – well, taken with them.

He looks hard at Pen, searching for symptoms. Pen raises an eyebrow.

What I am suggesting, he says, is that some students may ask for more help than others. Sometimes it is hard not to give them that help. But one must ensure parity.

Pen nods. Presses and presses the balls of her feet hard into the stirrups of chair legs, bracing.

Absolutely, she says. The issue of heightened student expectations has made many of us question where we are now to draw the line. Of course there must be a limit on how much we directly assist the students with research, but they expect a good deal more contact time now. It seems only fair in light of constant fee increases.

She hears her voice: high, metallic. Panicked. Swallows.

Yes, yes, Laurence says, rubbing an ear. Student expectation is a complex issue, of course—

I've been discussing the situation with Mary Dene, Pen says. And Steve. Mary is putting together a paper for the next faculty learning and teaching conference about this very issue.

Mary, he says. Yes. And Steve Saunders?

Yes, and Steve.

Laurence nods again, frowning. She waits.

She thinks: So. Was it Steve?

Someone. Someone spoke against her. She pictures meetings, naming of names, raising of hands.

She thinks: A disciplinary? She thinks: No. There is nothing they can use. Nothing. She has been careful. Perhaps some messages: perhaps. But nothing concrete. Only the mark is in question. Only that. Her wrists throb in her lap.

Well, Laurence says. You can understand my concern. But as far as I can see there is no further issue here. I will see to it that the paper in question is passed on to the external examiner in due course. But I doubt that the mark will be lowered.

I hope there will be no problem with it, Pen says. The student in question has applied to the MA and it would be a shame if his chances were reduced.

Indeed, Laurence says. Which MA?

Modernism, Pen says, swallowing the word.

Ah, he says. Well, thank you for your candour. I hope you don't mind my coming to see you.

I'm glad you did, she says. I understand your position completely.

He stands, shakes her hand, eyes scanning. She feels the dampness of palms, grips firmly. Smiles.

Nice shirt, by the way, she says. Very cheerful.

Thank you, he says. I thought it was rather splendid.

He leaves and Pen sits, breathes, stares through the window.

~

She makes tea in the staff kitchen. A sick hollow in her stomach. Someone passes in the corridor, slows, retraces. Appears in the doorway. Steve Saunders.

Penelope, he says.

She looks hard at him.

Are you all right? he says.

Fine, thank you, she says, bright, brittle. And you?

Hmm. Have you seen Laurence?

I saw him earlier, she says. You won't have any trouble spotting him. He's wearing a purple shirt.

Steve Saunders looks along the corridor. Removes his glasses, polishes the lenses on white shirt tail. Frowns.

Pen stamps onto the pedal of the bin, drops the spent teabag. Lets the lid squawk shut.

You? she says.

The word is hard, dry. He looks up. His face softens.

No, he says. Not me.

Who then?

A student.

Which one?

I don't know. He sighs. Christ, Penny, he says. Please be careful.

She takes him in, eyes wide brows joining, nose and cheeks naked, no glass no steel. He holds his hand out to her, glasses swinging. She thinks: Penny. She thinks: He knows then.

What? she says. What is it?

I haven't told a soul, he says. I swear I would never say anything.

Pen shakes her head. I don't know what you mean, she says.

Don't, he says. We've all been there. But times have changed. You know that. Any whiff of a scandal. Just please tell me you'll be more careful.

He replaces his glasses. Behind him the sound of doors, feet, passing students. Pen looks up: two girls. Not her students. Steve Saunders listens, waits, watches. Turns back to her.

Put an end to it, Penny, he says. Please. I'd hate to lose you.

Pen folds her arms. I don't know what you mean, Steve, she says.

He blinks at her, once, twice. Retreats.

Pen's vision reels. She carries tea back to her office, stares stupidly at the mug. She needs time to think; space. She phones Nate to let him know she will be late home. A woman answers. Pen leaves a message: Toby will be at his friend's house. Please ask Nate to pick him up after work.

Ringing off, she thinks: Who was that?

It is years since she has been to Nate's offices. Years since he visited her department. He could be anywhere, with anyone. They are surrounded by strangers.

She gathers folders, fills in online registers. Checks email. Watches as the windows darken, lights appear, shapes move in the rooms opposite.

She thinks: A student. A complaint. Close: too close.

She rereads Max's messages, checks them for warning signs. They scream of subtext. Every line is loaded: desire, anxiety, shared jokes. None of it on the surface. And yet. She thinks: Laurence, devotee of Barthes. Signs and signifiers. Laurence would know how to read through a message.

She could delete the emails. The cursor hovers. She thinks: Would that be worse? Panic, a sign of guilt. She thinks: It may not come to that. She thinks: The fleeing criminal, the dropped knife. Better to stay. Better to leave the words there, open, to brazen it out.

She should warn him. Max. But she cannot. She cannot call him. She dare not write. He is gone, home, seminars over, the long spring break. They have said their goodbyes, ten stolen minutes in her office, flinching at every sound. Still the hunger though, even then.

She thinks of it, feels the thought swell, filling her chest. Pushing out the sickness. She thinks: Keep it. Enjoy it. She thinks: Only Steve. Or are there? Others?

The tea is cold. She carries the mug back to the kitchen, empties it into the sink, stacks it in the dishwasher. The small white space hums. She needs to get outside, to walk, to shake it off. She gathers her things, locks the office, takes her bag to the car. She thinks: A walk in the darkness. She thinks: Does that look like guilt? She turns up the collar of her coat, locks the car, heads along the footpath towards the library.

Max knows not to write. They agreed it. Exam revision, the Stein book, family. Four weeks apart, a safe space. Then he will come and she will tell him. She edges around a puddle. The library glows, rows and rows of fluorescent squares, figures hurrying on the steps, a couple in the smoking shelter sharing a joint, the acrid stink of it as she passes. They look up to check Pen's expression and she nods, looks ahead, keeps on walking. She thinks: Has it begun to fall away a little? She thinks: Still the urgency, still the wanting. But a slow retreat beneath it. The dry rot of jealousy setting in. He of her world, of her constant refusals, of the need for secrecy. It is mostly unsaid but she feels it hover between them. Does he imagine a sophisticated life? Does he want to be part of it? But he is gone and she knows nothing about what he does beyond that. Does not want to know. Behind her the smoking couple murmur, the boy laughs softly and for a moment it freezes her, that laugh, that low youthful sound, and she thinks: We cannot go on. She thinks: I will lose him. He will find someone else. The path beneath her tilts and she swallows hard against a rising sickness, veers away behind a clump of trees, out of sight of the path, bends at the waist to bring the blood back to her head and everything swims, pulses, warps.

She straightens up, checks the path, the bulges of lamplight. No one has seen her. She walks the long way back to the car, the tick of her feet against the path a counting down. She thinks: Stein. The book fills the gaps. It is what she must use.

She is at the conclusion now. The editors probing, prompting her for pages. Then the final draft; line edits. Holding text in the catalogue. If she can make it, publication after Christmas. She cannot let this stall her, let the schedule slip. She must work. It was going so well, fuelled by that quickness, that sharp lucidity. She thinks: Max. She thinks: The MA. The first panel meeting at the end of next month. She cannot, now. Dare not. She thinks: He must be placed with someone else, a different tutor. Not the Modernism course. American Lit perhaps. She will tell him. He can change his mind. It often happens. She thinks: Will Laurence be looking? Would that be worse? She thinks: How can I? She thinks: And yet. If not. How would we?

She thinks: We would have to find another way. Or find an ending. Her mouth dries, sours. She cannot think of that. Not yet.

~

Pen stays away from campus. She cannot bear to see Steve Saunders, to bump into Laurence, to be in her office. She avoids checking email. After a day of editing she goes straight to Toby's end-of-term swimming meet. No phone calls. No ominous post.

She drives to the pool, parks, sits at the wheel. The motor hums. By the bins at the side of the building a woman, yellow hair in scraped ponytail, smoking. Knees flexing. The woman turns her back to the car park, wave insignia on blue T-shirt, flicks away the cigarette end. Pen watches the arc and fall. The woman reaches, hands clasped above her head, pushes hips from side to side. Retreats into the building through a side door. Pen sits.

She wills herself to move. Toby, sullen, asked this morning if she would be there. His face hidden by the clutter of cereal boxes. His voice pleading. Pen reaches across the passenger seat, clears files into the back. Turning she sees Natalie Matthews, fingers in hair, torso rising between parked cars. Pen could catch her. She retrieves her bag, swings open the door, slams, locks. Natalie nears the automatic glass doors, Pen hard behind her. She thinks: Jack Matthews. Toby has avoided the name for weeks. Pen has voiced suspicions sotto voce but Toby's silence is unyielding.

Natalie is already far into the raked seats, talking with another woman. The woman stands, leans beside her, backcombed hair nesting high on head, black leggings, pink point-toed heels. Giant fake fur collar. Pen thinks: How long does it take to create this fiction? Surely she cannot have a child, cannot be doing the morning run, cannot have a husband that leaves mid-breakfast, the worst of the battle of hair-combing and bag-packing still to be done. Pen cannot imagine such luxury. Pen edges along the seats towards them but there is something, a hardness, holding her back. She practises what she might say to Natalie, her fears about Jack and Toby, such a shame, friends for years, do you know anything about it? Pen stares at the woman with the hair, the splayed spiders of false eyelashes. Cannot move.

She sits, turns away, watches the swimmers. Tries to make out Toby but they are all the same, these boys, gangly, hunched, hair one wet colour flat against scalps. At ease only in the water. Pen thinks: Intimidated. Ashamed of the body, awed by the bodies of others. She thinks: I too, of this woman, of her plasticity, her sheer effort. She thinks: When did it happen? When did I become other, the enemy? She thinks of Max again, of Steve's plea to be careful. Put an end to it. She pushes the thought away.

As soon as the heats are over Pen escapes, sidles out before Natalie can see her, sits in the foyer sipping a paper cone of water. Toby comes out ahead of the others, head down, drawstring bag swaying, damp hair curling. Barely a smile. Pen offers a pizza restaurant, lures to extend the evening, but all he wants is home, the shell of his room. She is certain then: there is hostility, bullying perhaps, a feud. Easier to talk to him in the car, her eyes on the road, his face averted. She probes, tests, mentions Jack Matthews. And there it is: Toby and Jack and a girl between them, threats, humiliations. She thinks: A girl? Already. Pen flinches with it, her boy hurting, the first souring of friendship. First hormonal rivalry. The girl unnamed. The power of the unpronounced, *so much and yet more silence*. Pointless to tell him that it will pass. Pointless to try. She thinks of it, shapes the words but does not release them: Jack will still be there when this girl is gone, Jack will grow up, you will grow up, you are both in thrall and she will probably never want either of you and in six months you will not care.

Instead she says: I saw Jack's mother talking to someone.

Big hair? says Toby.

That's the one.

Oh, he says. That's Jayden Taylor's mum.

Pen senses tribal politics. Flicks eyes at Toby. Jayden? she says. What kind of name is that?

Toby laughs. Pouts. The name of the boy that girls *do* like, he says.

Nonsense, Pen says. His name is Toby.

He says nothing, turns away, eyes on passing shopfronts. She thinks: So then. So it begins.

That evening, Toby asleep, she unpacks her bags, piles folders, arranges the study. She will finish the Stein book. She is ready. She must sweep away all obstacles. She slides the Hemingway book back on the shelf, parting the gap with chipped spine, the pale face on the cover slotting into place. She has not chosen her next project, not allowed herself to think of it. Six weeks, two months perhaps. A respite. Then she can decide. When the Stein book is done she will change her reading diet. There are piles of books she has put aside, novels she has longed to climb into. It is time now. She will luxuriate, escape elsewhere.

In the kitchen she makes tea, puts out the bins, carries the compost caddy to the heap at the bottom of the garden. It is late but already the quality of light is changing. The grass feels spongy beneath her, the air tastes of spring: metallic, resinous. She knows it now, feels it with absolute clarity. Toxicity in her gut, in her limbs. Steve is right. She will have to let Max go, however it feels. Make him go.

He, Ernest, has unhinged you now. You are no longer rational. And you are devious, spiteful. A devil. He takes David and Marita away from you and when they are not looking, makes you his wrecking ball.

What is he afraid of? Why is he so angry?

You find out. You are in the hotel bedroom. You are looking for something. When you find it you close it in your hand and leave, walk along the corridor. Your step is quick, determined. You come to David's room, the one he uses to write in. You open your hand. There is a key in it. You unlock the door, step inside; soft, soft. Close it behind you.

Your tread is light. You go to the desk but it is empty. Beneath it is a suitcase; you pick it up, lay it on the bed, open it. Inside are David's notebooks. There are several of them in a pile, the sort that French schoolchildren write their grammar exercises in. You take these out, flick through them. Yes, these are the stories, the ones David has been writing. There are others, with the story of you in them, the story Ernest has been writing. You move these aside. They are safe. There are pencils, of course, and some large, wadded envelopes. You take out the envelopes.

What are you doing? What would he have you do?

You close the suitcase and put it back under the desk, gather the notebooks and envelopes under your arm. You scan the room. Nothing else is of interest to you. The bed has never been slept in: David prefers Marita's room. Perhaps he, David, Ernest, thinks this is somehow more gallant. The room joins onto Marita's. It is certainly convenient.

You leave, lock the door behind you, return the key to your room. Then you go down through the hotel and the side door, around the garden, into the yard where Madame sees to the laundry and where the bicycles that you and David once rode so often and so well are stored, their tires flattening from disuse.

Ernest is fast inside you now. You feel his hand on you like a slap. He maneuvres you so surely, so definitely, that your body is tense, muscular. Inside you are treading water, letting the tide do the work. Your hands move objects with such rapidity that the air around you blurs. Here is the burner. You move it toward you. There is gasoline in a can on a shelf. You place the notebooks in a neat fan inside the burner. You empty the envelopes on top, a sprinkling of clippings. A strong sousing of gasoline. There is a book of matches in your pocket. You have come prepared.

The fire is quick to start. This is cheap paper, after all. The clippings are heavy with ink and take a while, curling at the edges, burning toward their centers. You watch as the notebooks char, flame, soften. You find a large stick and stir the ash, breaking the gray leaves. There is a faint trace of ink on some, the ghost of ruled lines. The pencil marks are erased, though. That is what

matters. Even the covers of the notebooks are stirred into fragments the size of postage stamps.

You stand at the burner. The ash cools. It twitches in the faint
breeze. Smell the smoke in the air, the acrid taste of it in your throat.
You feel him, Ernest, shaking inside you. It is as if he is sobbing.

Something has happened to him. Something like this.

What, though? Did someone take his writing, his, Ernest's, and
destroy it? Is it that? Or is he angry at something else, someone
else? You try to ask him.

Call him, now. What does he want of you? Why is he treating
you like this? Is he accusing you?

No. It is not you. You are a vehicle; that is all. This is an
exorcism.

You continue to stand there. Now you are still you can take in
all the details: the spokes of the bicycle wheels, a rusted lawn-
mower, a piece of broken machinery raised on bricks. There is
tarpaulin shouldered over a humped shape, green, mildewed in
the corner where the triangular point dips above a shallow pit
and rain must pool in the winter. A small cluster of nettles have
sprung up behind an iron gate.

You can feel Ernest watching you. He is dwelling in this. He
is shaping every inch of the space around you. He is breathing
it in and out of himself as you breathe it. You are the same. You
are in his thoughts now and he in yours and you and he are
one and the same.

Yes. That's the difference. He hasn't written down a single
word of it.

~

David is calm when you tell him. You expected him to rage,
to throw things. That would be refreshing. But no, not he. He
reacts as if someone has died. He asks to see the body. You tell
him about the burner, the stick, the ash. He nods. He leaves you
at the bar and when he comes back you can smell the coarse
scent of smoke on him. He has been raking through the ashes.
He will not find anything useful there; you made sure of that.
You and Ernest.

After a death there are formalities. There is a will. Monies are
paid out. There are solicitors.

If David is going to behave like that then you will play along.
You tell him how glad you are that he is behaving reasonably.
He tells you that he would like to kill you but that he won't,
because you are ill. Yes, that card again. Marita looks at you
with those sorrowful eyes and it is all you can do not to scream.
Instead you say you will pay David for his stories. You will go
to Paris and talk to your lawyers about it. David drinks a large
whiskey and soda. This is when he lets down his guard. He
rants at you. He, David, Ernest, says that he wishes he had never
met you, that your mother had never met your father, that he
regrets everything you have ever done together.

Do not let David, Ernest, draw you into a fight. Remain calm.

229

You will have your moment.

This is how: leave them. Go.

You wait until they have left, David and Marita, in the Bugatti. You have told them you will drive to Paris in the morning. They take the car. You will not wait for the car. You will not wait for them. You will take the train.

David and Marita will be relieved when you have gone. They will eat supper and drink champagne and conspire about their future. Madame too. She has always preferred Marita to you. Perhaps the women will coerce David into new patterns. You have given him his freedom, but Marita is different. There is something else beneath that hollow shine, that reflection she holds up to dazzle David. Yes, she will not settle for the passive role of reader, not forever. If you are gone then Ernest will turn to Marita. He cannot do without a woman for long. She may get bolder, start to take over, interfere with his writing. David, Ernest, may allow her to. Yes, you like this idea. David losing his voice. Marita gaining hers.

And then what? Ernest may bring you back, in time. But if you have your way, this is goodbye.

11.

On the first day back Pen sees Max in a corridor. She is brief, businesslike. Stay away, she says. She does not let herself look at him. She cannot be his tutor again, she tells him, saying it to the poster behind his head, the red font she cannot read, the image of a horse or a deer or something four-legged and slight hovering in her vision. When she is done she looks hard at drawing pins and spent staples patterning the hardboard wall, the handwritten adverts for rooms to let, the UniSoc gatherings, double shots on Tuesdays. *Giving it away not giving it away.* Max pleads in low tones, hand reaching for her sleeve: Why are you doing this what have I done why now? Penelope? She tries not to hear him. *Is there any difference.*

Compromise, she says. Complaint. No, she will not let him into the office. No, they cannot talk about it, cannot wait it out. Max shakes his head, stares at her dumbly, unyielding. Pen lets herself see him briefly, that mouth. Wreckage in his face. She thinks: I must not yield I must not. Walks away, soles of her feet burning, holding her sides, willing the seams not to weaken, eyes, *any little thing is water.*

She hurls herself into exile, doesn't leave the house, out of office reply on the email. Frenetic writing and rereading and revising into the early hours. Blinkers on. Shuttered, cloistered. Leaves Nate to deal with Toby. Barely washes or eats or sleeps.

Within a week the Stein book is done: a catharsis. Pen sends the final draft to the editors. That night she and Nate share a bottle of Moët. She almost confesses, undone by Nate's small gestures of approval, by her own hollowness, by the bewildering effort of celebration. They have sex on the sofa. It surprises them both. Pen wakes in the morning dry-mouthed, acid in her stomach, the displaced sense as she comes to consciousness that something or someone has died in a shocking mutilation. She looks at herself in the mirror, the hard emptiness of face, hair stringy, growing out over the ears. She is uncertain how or when to mourn. Grief hangs above her, an umbrella, the tips of its spokes a constant periphery.

When she returns to the office there are notes from Max, folded scraps of pleading pushed under the door. The cleaners have not been in. On the email a single message, the moment of David Bourne's remorse: *His chest felt as though there were an iron bar inside it from one side to the other.* Pen paces; considers replies; deletes it. She feels him on every surface, in every fibre of the room.

She moves, a stunned thing, through the last empty weeks of term. Max is in each tall shape she passes, in the scent of grass cuttings, in the gait of supermarket strangers. Clinging to her clothes. She tries to smarten up, gets her hair trimmed, buys a new dress. Token efforts of reinvention. Despite herself, despite all sense, longing strikes, an inward thrashing. Sudden pulses of adrenaline, hot rushes of remembrance, cutting through everything: eating dinner, taking a shower, talking to her neighbour as he puts out the bins. They come in waves, crashing through her, unannounced. She has no defence against them. The smell of Max, the sweet greenness. His eyes eyelids heavy blue and black and desire swimming. Softness and bending limbs, a pulling together. Vertiginous. Aftershocks that rock her until she can barely stand, barely keep herself from crying out. She had this: she gave this away. How? Why? She thinks: Come back come back please. Come back to me. She thinks: I could reach him. Seek him. He would come. She thinks: Put an end to it. And she did. She had to. But oh, the waste of it, the recklessness of this ending. How she could throw herself away now, drive herself, like the ghost of Catherine Bourne, over the cliff and into the sea.

1958: Ketchum

The woods were cool and the leaves were already collecting in the ruts of earth where the track cut through. There was dew on the leaves and on the toes of his boots as he walked. It was only just light but today he needed to walk before he started work. He walked away from the lodge and he could hear the pigeons that gathered on the roof calling through the woods behind him.

His chest wheezed a little as he walked. He wasn't an old man yet but he felt it. The plane crashes and the sickness had made an old man of him. He had been forty-seven when he started the Riviera novel and in the summer he would be sixty. His beard was white now and when he awoke in the mornings his hands shook. His back was stiff and sore and on bad days the pain sprang up from his kidneys and shot through his spine. He took sedatives and vitamins and steroids. He was on pills for his heart and pills for his liver and kidneys. His moods were black most of the time now and the doctor had given him antidepressants and tranquilizers. Kittner and the doctor had made him go for a year without hard liquor but he hadn't felt any better for it. Now at least he was back on the whiskey again. He needed that to take the edge off things.

He rubbed his hands together and curled his fingers into the cuffs of his coat. The cold felt good but he was glad of the fur on his collar.

It had been a hot crazy summer in Cuba. The fishing was bad and the air was thick. There were black specks of midges on the billiard table and on some mornings they made a crust of insect bodies that floated on the pool like scum in a bathtub. The heat made it hard to work but he had still managed it, standing at the typewriter to ease his back, his shirt soaked through by noon. He'd grown sick of the heat inside the Finca, the shades drawn in the tower room and the boat waiting, a free pass, by the jetty. And then no fish however long he stayed out. The heat had ruined everything.

He was glad to get away from Cuba with the heat and the revolution gnawing at the government and setting everyone on edge. There had been break-ins at the Finca and once he'd surprised a group of thieves in the grounds. He'd shot his rifle at them as they ran and clipped one of them in the shoulder. Another night he'd been woken by guards demanding a house search. The housekeeper called him down and he went to the door. The chief of the guards accused him of hiding revolutionaries and building a stockade in the basement. The housekeeper was pale and Kittner appeared and looked sick but he toughed it out. He told the guard he was an honest American citizen and that he had no other political allegiances and that their countries held each other in mutual respect. The guards did not search the Finca but even so he did not sleep well that night. In the morning the gardener came to tell him that one of the dogs was dead. The gardener had found him on the path with his head smashed. After that he had slept even less and he and Kittner agreed it might be wise to get out of Cuba for a while.

He had no love for the Cuban government and he was hopeful for Castro and the socialist uprising. Even so it was a bad time to be a rich American in a villa in the country. He and his wife packed up their things and closed the Finca and took the lodge and the house in Ketchum.

He walked on, cutting a circuit through the woods around the lodge. He would not walk too far in case he jarred his back and caused more trouble for himself. Rounding the bend toward the woodshed he surprised a couple of snipe. He stopped to listen to the sound of their wings cutting through the dry October air.

As he walked he thought about the memoir. He had worked steadily on it but he was having trouble finishing. He had all the sketches of life in Paris, of meeting Scott and of Ford and Pound and visiting Gertrude and Alice at number 27. He had these little slices and they fit together well but what he lacked was an ending. He hadn't thought of a title either. Titles were the toughest part. Maybe if he left the book for a while it would find its own ending. Sometimes the further away he was from something the better he could see it. Stepping back was a good thing. Working on the novel should be like that too. He knew that when Monet worked on his last great paintings he needed a warehouse for a studio. It wasn't just the case of housing a thing that size. It was getting enough distance to take it in at once.

Well, he'd given the Riviera novel plenty of distance. He'd picked it up and put it down and worked hard at it and boxed it away for months at a time. He'd been working on it for years now and he felt it would be his last big landscape. He knew that if he wanted it to work like the Monet paintings he needed to focus the action. The paintings were huge but the focus in them narrow and the strokes broad. The water in the paintings showed something of what was above but also spoke of what was underneath. It was important to suggest things and not just show them. There should be depth but some of that depth must be hidden. He agreed with Monet on that too.

He could cover a lot of ground in the story by sticking to a few places. That was how the memoir was working. Instead of writing about everything he'd done and everywhere he'd been he'd stuck to Paris. The problem with the Riviera idea was that there were too many scenes and too many characters. If he could strip it down to the story of David the young American writer and his marriage and his lover then he would have enough for a novel. But the cutting wasn't easy.

He walked the track to the woodshed. The pheasants were hanging there and he wanted to check on them.

He knew he needed to pare the material right back if he was going to make a novel out of it but that didn't help him. Every day he wrote a little more and the thing swelled and took on its own life. That was the way it had been since he'd started making money. When he was poor in Paris and after that with the early books he was disciplined and had no trouble cutting. Now the books he worked on had no deadlines and he didn't need to worry about the money coming in. He could work on several at once and if he needed any money he could do an article or an essay, or write an introduction for something. It was a whole different world to Paris.

When the memoir came out he would be able to forget about Paris and by then he would have the Riviera novel finished too. Maybe after that he would think about an African book again. He had enough on Africa to fill two novels and he had packed away that script and put it in the vault in Cuba. The remains of the big war book were there too. He had taken much of that apart now but there was still plenty left. It was vast but then everything was vaster than it should have been. Everything was spiraling away from him and he knew it.

He pushed the door and went into the shed. The logs were stacked neatly to the sides. There was good timber there and when it burned in the fires in the lodge the smoke had a fine clean smell to it. The pheasants were hanging at the back of the shed and he checked the feel and the weight of each of them to see how they were drying. The small chestnut feathers were soft on the birds' breasts. The pheasants' green and white necks were stretched and their bodies swung gently toward each other as he felt them. It would be fine to have pheasant for supper soon but he didn't want to rush them. The birds were best when they'd hung for a good long while and were tender and rich and gamey.

He was working steadily on the Riviera idea. He'd thought for a while that it would never be published, or that it would have to wait until he was dead. He'd doubted Scribner's would touch it. Then he'd read Nabokov's book and he was not so worried.

The African material was rough though. He knew the publishers would never print the language he used and without the language the book would fall apart. The language was part of the coarseness of the lives lived in the book and modifying it or tuning it down would make those lives and voices empty. An African book would have to wait. But the Riviera novel had scope now.

He left the pheasants in the woodshed and pulled the door hard behind him. He was enjoying the pheasant season but the winter would be fine with him too. When the snows came they would leave the lodge and settle in the Ketchum house. There would be fires and suppers in the house and quiet evenings. Maybe then his wife would calm down a little and give him some peace.

He had not shown Kittner the Riviera novel. He wasn't ready to share it with her yet. He knew she would see a good deal of herself in it and their experiments in bed too and he knew what she would have to say about putting that in a book. She wouldn't like what he was doing to the character of the writer's wife and there was plenty about his own wives that Kittner might not like either. Instead he gave her the proofs of his memoir to type. It kept her busy and made her feel involved. He wasn't worried that in the memoir he wrote about Wicky and how much he loved her. Kittner could deal with that. She had dealt with worse.

He walked on around the track and back up toward the lodge. He had rowed with Kittner again the night before. She liked to row with him at the end of the day when his wits were slower. Many times lately she had complained and said he was out of control, that she would leave him, that he didn't deserve her or anyone else that cared about him. Sometimes he knew it, knew he was doing it, his head all turned around and filled up with the pettiness and spite of living with and tolerating others. When he wasn't free to work and didn't have the necessary clarity he felt hooked and dragged like one of the great marlin he caught out on the Gulf, lifted up and out and left thrashing on the deck. He couldn't help it if his wife got in the way when he was like that. In this latest row she had told him he neglected her and he answered that she was doing her best to damage his work and interrupt his writing. She said he was drinking too much and he cursed and threw his glass at her and raised his fists. So she screamed and turned her back on him and went straight to bed. When he went in later he had found the note she left for him. *You are a selfish bastard, Papa*, it said, *but I love you, damn you. Get some sleep.*

Up and down with her, up and down. She could be a nurse and a friend and then the wrong look in the wrong direction and she was a harpy. He had given her a hard time with other women they had both known and mixed with, and with that young whore in Havana and the Venetian girl and even the Wakamba girl Debba, but he was through with that now. Every time he'd looked at a girl it had started Kittner up again. Neglect, she'd said. At least while they were out here there were no women to distract him or upset her. There was just the writing and the woods and the men coming over in the afternoons to shoot pheasant.

He was done with jealousy but he was not done with writing it. There was plenty of that in the Riviera novel. David's wife was jealous of his lover but worse was her jealousy of his writing. This was the real problem between them and he had known it at the beginning. He wanted to show in the book how hard it was for a writer to keep this balance. A writer had to be true to his work but he also had a responsibility to his wife. If he neglected one or the other his world was damaged. If he gave too much to his work his marriage would fail. If he gave too much to his marriage his career would suffer and his writing would be compromised. That was why he was now so sure of the ending. If the wife left, the young writer David would still have his lover and his work. If she stayed his career would be all washed up. So she must come back. Knowing this, the writer would be willing to end his own life. It would please David's devil wife to know his writing would not survive her. She would ask this of him. If she were to become too ill for him to care for her or for her to know herself they would kill themselves. They would promise this to each other. It did not matter how they went about it because the book would not see things through that far. The important thing was for the reader to know that the writer's work and the wife's sanity could not outlast each other and that while they seemed healthy enough they could both come to a sudden end.

That was still how he wanted it to be. It would be a quiet suffocation of an ending.

He opened the door of the lodge and kicked off his boots. At least he had an ending even if he was having trouble steering the story at it. If he died before it was finished he hoped to hell the bastards wouldn't take that out. He'd already seen Hollywood destroy his Kilimanjaro story, giving the dying writer with the rotting leg a way out and a happy ending. Bastards. There were no happy endings.

He hung up his coat. Thank Christ Hollywood had finished shooting their film of his fisherman story. He would sue them if they used a rubber marlin after all his work.

The lodge was warm and he could hear the housekeeper stacking logs in the big fireplace. The fire in his room would already be lit. He put his head around the door and asked the housekeeper for some coffee.

Of course, she said, right away. She was kneeling by the fireplace and emptying the log basket. Are you ready for some breakfast, Papa? she said.

No, he said, I'll work now. I took a walk to check on the pheasants.

They must be ready, she said. Would you like one tonight?

Not yet, he said. Give them a few more days to hang.

I'll bring you some coffee, she said. Won't you take some eggs at least? Or some toast?

No, Daughter, he said. Just the coffee.

He headed to his work room. Whatever Hollywood did to it, the fisherman story was a fine book and he'd written every word in it as pure and clean as it could be. He knew at the time it was the finest thing he had written and that no one had been as pure with language since Shakespeare. Christ, listen to that. What bull. That was the kind of thing Stein used to say. Still, it was true he'd taken every word in that story and stripped it down with his pen like you'd whittle a stick with a knife till the clean sap showed through.

That was what he needed to do to the Riviera novel.

He looked at the pile on his desk. He would put in another story for the writer's wife to be jealous of and disgusted by. He needed to show how clearly and sharply their worlds were dividing. Only by doing this would the suffocation of the ending be truly terrible.

David's story would be hard for him to write but it would be a story he'd been avoiding and wanting in equal measure. It would be about his childhood in Africa again, and the father he admired and despised.

~

He started shaping the scene. The young writer poured himself a whiskey and soda and added some ice and sat down at the small bar in the hotel.

Damn him, he thought. Damn him with his drink and his women and his story ready to be told and no one waiting for him to fall or hoping that he would. Damn that. He needed to sit at a bar with a whiskey and soda too. But he was in a lodge in the woods on an October morning and not in a hotel in the Riviera in the afternoon sunshine, and he had only just started working.

So what about that? He could have a whiskey without the soda, to warm him through.

He knew what. If he drank now the work would suffer. He was on a good diet again and he was walking in the woods and keeping his weight steady. He needed to hold himself down. He was ready to write the thing now.

He could really do with that coffee.

He got up and stood by the door and listened for the house-keeper. He could go into the kitchen and tell her to hurry up.

He had only just spoken to her. He needed to settle down.

He would have a drink later, like the writer with his ice and soda and the morning's work done. He could wait until lunchtime.

He went back to his desk and started in on the story again. The writer David had finished the African story and sat at the bar to drink his whiskey and soda and think about his father.

The housekeeper nudged the door open and put down a tray of coffee. He nodded but did not look up. He heard the door close again behind him.

The American writer's lover came in and sat next to him at the bar. She asked him how the work had been. When he told her that he had finished she asked to read the story and he gave her the key. She fetched the notebook from his room and sat at the bar reading the story. When she finished she told him how good it was and how finely he had written about the country. Later his wife came in and found out about the girl reading the story and was furious. She was happy for the girl to sleep with her husband but reading his stories was another thing. The writer's wife never read his stories, she said, but provided him with the means to write them. The writer made jokes and the girl protested. In the end the wife read half the story and ripped apart the notebook in disgust.

When he finished writing the scene he was quietly pleased but not ready to read it through again. He picked up the pot of coffee and poured himself a cup. He looked down at the page and found himself back in the final passage of the story. The writer's wife was arch and high-handed and it was clear she was becoming unhinged. Whether she liked the story or not her voice and her actions showed how she was losing control. He had been careful only to hint at her madness through small outbursts. He hoped that by showing the girl's shock and the writer's self-control it would be enough.

He put away the script and sat down to drink his coffee. He had swallowed half of it before he realized it was cold. In the hall outside the clock began to chime. The chimes went on and on. When he counted the eleventh chime he got up and went into the big room and poured himself a whiskey and brought it back to his desk.

He opened the desk drawer and took out the script of his memoir. He leafed through the pages and made some slight corrections in pencil. Then he set the pages next to the type-writer for Kittner to read.

He sipped his whiskey and looked at the pages and wondered how it had come to this. In his memoir he was cruel and sarcastic and he had eulogized his first wife but that was all fine. Kittner could read it and if he got it into shape his publishers would print it. But his fiction was dangerous. The Riviera novel was shut away in a case under the desk. He did not want his wife to read it. He was not sure if anyone would ever read it.

He leaned back in his chair and smiled. It seemed right somehow. The story of the young writer David was truer than his memoir could ever be. It was too true to print.

You sit at the desk in the hotel room. You have only this one act. You will make something to leave behind and you will not do it with a pencil and the lined pages of a cheap, schoolboy's notebook. You take out your fountain pen and writing paper. The paper is dense, smooth, ivory. You unscrew the lid of the pen. It is light in your hand. Your writing is fluid. It surprises you, this writing, but then you have never seen it before. Ernest has only ever given you letters to read. When you reply it is offstage, unseen, unwritten.

So you write. It is only a letter, but you have learned some tricks. David, Ernest, cannot keep a secret. You jump straight into metaphor, extend it, give it a truth of its own. The car crash of you. The killing of his infant stories. It is apt, although you do not say so; the notebooks were childish.

You offer an explanation, the one Ernest wants you to give. Is that all right with you? A compromise? But why not, you think. It is not a compromise. It is a collaboration.

It is a short letter, but it is enough. It will be there when you are not. David, Ernest, cannot unmake it. You will be free.

You sign the letter, put it in an envelope, mark it for David's attention. You put some things in a case: clothes, books, toothbrush, powder, face creams, soap. The evening is cool now. You slip on your jacket, take the case, shut the door without a backward glance.

When they come back, you are gone.

12.

Pen avoids the summer graduation ceremony, offers instead to host the drinks reception, fruit punch, crates of too-warm wine and white paper tablecloths, two women from Catering wheeling a trolley across the lawn. In the shade of the marquee she watches students sweep towards her, gowns and mortar boards, oversized envelopes under arms, some in pairs, some with family. She tries not to scan for Max but sees him in every approaching figure, her eyes restless across spaces: bottles jugs tables pegs ropes lawn. The path beyond filling with bodies, boys scrubbed and suited, girls polished and teetering in their heels, parents proud and swollen or shrinking and out of depth. Busies herself with cups, returns small waves, nods encouragement. Smiles, shakes hands, congratulates. Longs to see him, to glimpse him. Fears it. Searches faces until she finds him.

Max. Across the lawn, dark suit, white shirt, open collar, mortar board under one arm, nodding and talking to someone. Who? She shifts aside to see. Jay Fisher. Max turns to a man beside him who clasps his shoulder, shakes Jay Fisher's hand, a man with dark hair, silvering, shorter than Max but she knows this must be his father and she turns away, unsteady, excuses herself, feigning a summons. Retreats to the marquee's edge. Watches as Max approaches, sees her, halts. Pen nods, looks towards her office. Wills him to understand. He passes her in a wide arc and joins the drinks queue.

Pen tells Freddie Mann she's expecting a call and leaves for her office, promising to return. Sits at the desk smoothing hands on silk, waiting it out. She thinks: He saw me, understood me. She thinks: He will come.

Pen waits. Stands at the window; checks the corridor. She thinks: He is not coming.

She sits again, stares at the desk, the untouched page proofs of her Stein book, the corkboard clutter of pinned tasks and calls for papers. Hears the door at the far end of the corridor click and sigh, the sounds of movement approaching. A knock. She swallows hard.

Come in, she says.

Max opens the door. He picks one of the hard chairs lined against the wall, angles it towards her. Sits, an acre of carpet rolling out between them, long legs rigid in formal trousers. Intractable. From the corner of an eye she sees the door ajar, the narrow strip of corridor; escape route. Max leans back, tips his head, enquiring.

Max, she says. Her mouth aches with the name. It's good to see you.

How are things? he says.

She wants to say that she's unnerved, no, terrified: of herself, of him, of doing more damage, of a reckoning.

I'm okay, she says. How are you?

I'm fine.

Pen takes him in, his angular politeness, the set of his shoulders. She thinks: What did I expect? She thinks: Is he waiting for something – or waiting to strike? She thinks: I could go to him, right now, get up from this chair and round the desk and break everything, start it all again, touch that face, plead forgiveness.

Max, she says. Are you angry with me?

Why?

Because I wouldn't see you. I'm sorry if you felt ignored.

Max folds his arms. Things move on, don't they? he says.

No, she wants to say, no, there is only displacement, there is only spiralling and repetition and a slow weakening. Resignation.

So, you have your first, she says. Congratulations.

Thanks.

What next?

I'm not taking up the MA place.

I know, she says. I'm on the panel. I see all the applications.

Oh, he says.

So what will you do?

I'm planning to study in the States. I'm applying for a scholarship.

Something subsides within Pen, turns to water. She braces herself against it, the hammering of sea wall, the shameful mess of broken defences.

Well, she says. That's − exciting.

Dr Saunders is helping me with my application. It's very competitive, but he says that with my grades, and strong references from him and the Head of School, I stand a good chance.

Pen thinks: Steve Saunders. Of course. Always Steve. And now Laurence.

She crosses her legs, braces hands over knees. Max speaks. She makes out odd words: opportunity, realistic, direction. She thinks: Target words. Angular. Consonant. A wall of them. She thinks: What of sibilance, of smooth hushing, of softness? What of alliterative lilting? Lover. Leaving. Loss.

Pen looks at the door, the gap, the distance. Beautiful boy. Goodbye and goodbye and goodbye. Clears her throat. Max, she says, to the space above his ear, the cruel corner of steel picture frame. Holding it down.

You must know how sorry I am that we're losing you, she says. I know you have good reason to move on, shed a skin. That perhaps you feel you've outgrown your surroundings and we have nothing left to offer you.

She hears her own words from a distance: damaging unmeant words of not-self, now-knotted self.

But there are other MA options here, she says. Research degrees. You could have chosen to work with a supervisor. It's not too late, if the funding doesn't work out. I could put in a recommendation. There would be no lack of support for you, if you wanted to stay.

Max frowns. Stay here? he says. Really? I don't think so.

Her eyes skate across his. He looks away.

I understand, she says.

Look, he says. I should really go back outside. My parents are here.

Of course, she says.

Max stands, moves towards her, hand outstretched. Pen stands to meet him, takes it, this hand, his hand, retreating now; holds it between her palms, feels the slim length of a finger, the softly rounded pad. No longer hers.

Oh, Max, she says. You can't imagine how—

I can, he says. I mean, I did too.

She thinks: Past tense. This is no farewell. He has already left her behind, bobbing in his wake. Flotsam.

I'd better go, he says.

Yes, she says. Join your family. Enjoy your day.

Thanks, he says.

Good luck, Max.

See you then, he says. Maybe.

He moves away, hand swinging loose at his side, fingers curling. She watches the movement, angles described on carpet, air displaced, swing of door, a solid mass, ushered open. Closed. The sounds of leaving. She does not look up.

The waters rise and roar: a sound from the corner of the room. Pen listens to it, a soft keening, a stoppered howl, tries to place the source of it. Realises she is the source. She holds a hand over her mouth.

Pen moves without sense, through the empty corridor, fire-escape door propped with blue plastic chair, two paper cups balancing on the step, pink slush spillage of macerated fruit, tall student, *not him*, blonde-haired, smoking behind a pillar, grey suit-sleeve parting black wing of gown, across the lawn the hum of the reception, of distant voices calling, squealing, of leave-taking. She moves beyond it, against the walls of buildings, willing herself not to be seen, to round the corner to the car park before she is noticed, before Freddie Mann turns, before Laurence waves to her, before someone calls her back.

~

Only when there is distance, a queue of cars at the roundabout, the flickering lights of the level crossing: only then. Pen swings the wheel, turns away from town and out to the coast, climbs out of the sound and the tremors of the body and crests the hill, past houses and schools and pub signs, farm shops, weather vanes, succession of neatly threaded villages, flashes of passing windscreens, green tunnels of hedgerow, incongruous midsummer sunshine beating her eyelids.

Pen turns into a clearing in the woods: empty gravelled car park, maze of wooden climbing frame, mossy picnic benches. She sits and listens to the keening sound, the rising, the dry heaving of breath seeking passage, forcing itself into the spaces between her limbs, the shell of the car. Leans into the wheel, arms rigid, eyes cheeks hands throat shameful, raw. Howls and howls and howls.

When she has finally done with crying it is nearly dark. She drives home.

My God, says Nate. You look beaten.

Migraine, she says. I feel awful.

All that ceremony, he says. Did they get emotional at you? Did something happen with a student?

Almost, she says.

There's always one, Nate says. You'd better lie down.

She thinks: Again, the nearness of it, the suicide-leap of confession. She removes shoes and jacket, lies on the bed. Lapses, somehow, into sleep. Wakes to find Nate beside her gently easing a mug onto the bedside table: Ginger tea, he says. Toby sits beside her in pyjamas smelling of soap powder and pinewood, of open-air laundering, kisses her a round-eyed goodnight. When she opens her eyes again it is still and dark, Nate in bed with sidelamp lowered, reading a magazine, Le Corbusier angular on the cover. Nate pauses, finger on printed page, leans to rub her temples, shoulders. She thinks: Tender. She thinks: I do not deserve tenderness.

Pen gets up to pee, vomits, hangs vampiric over the toilet bowl. Brushes teeth, drinks a mug of water by the kitchen sink. Undresses numbly. Climbing back into bed it comes to her again, that sound, threatens her chest until Nate switches off the light, flattens out beside her, breathing slowing, breaking into snores.

She presses into the pillow. In the dark she can make out shapes of furniture, of right-angled windowpanes behind curtains, of the lampshade like a mushroomed stain on the bedroom ceiling. Nate's jacket slung on the shoulder of a chair. Nate's hair, tea tree oil and warmth, like molten candle wax.

She thinks: Nate is a habit. She thinks: Bitter affection for a jacket on the back of a chair. Lapel curling. Smelling of custom. Smelling of comfortable use. She thinks: It could have been worse. Max is gone, gone, brittle at the end, caustic. She tastes the acid of his leaving, knows it will be there again tomorrow, that it will linger, this silent corrosion, eating steadily through weeks, months. But it could have been worse.

She thinks: What have I done? She thinks: Was it worth it? She thinks: Anything we can have and we had it. For a while. We did.

Sliding towards sleep she thinks not of Max or Nate but of all the people she knew at college and wanted but never acted, never took the leap. Why had she not invested in those possibilities, stored them up against nights like these? Faces in bars, beautiful faces, bent over library books, in stairwells, at bus stops, parties, train carriages, passing escalators. College nights of lying awake, dry-eyed, listening to the sound of the bed up-stairs thump against the radiator, the low moaning of another woman sounding down the corridors, a carolling, corralling consciousness, ceaseless spiralling and circling, trailing her like the endless echo of some terrible grief.

Gone. Gone. She closes the book of it with her eyelids, slides into the vortex.

1961: Ketchum

He had called himself an old man for a while now. It was a pose of sorts. One of many. In a couple of weeks he would turn sixty-two but he already knew he was as old now as he would ever get. His head ached. He sat up against the pillows and balled his hands into fists and screwed them into his temples.

He was glad to be back at the Ketchum house. He and Kittner and their friend George had eaten a good supper in the restaurant. It had been a fine warm day. George had driven them home across country from the clinic. He would not be going back there again.

There were lots of places he would not go back to. The Finca was lost to him. After the Bay of Pigs there could be no more Americans in Cuba. He had been supportive of Castro and had contacted him when he first came to power and offered his advice. Now the Finca would be overrun. The Cuban government were taking back everything the Americans had. He had lost his library and his pictures and everything they had not packed up and brought away with them. He had probably lost the African script and the remains of the big war book left in the vault there.

Maybe they would find the manuscripts when he was gone. If they did he hoped to hell they published every filthy bloody word of them.

He got out of bed. Kittner was asleep in her room. He paused in the hallway and listened to her snoring. They did not share a bedroom anymore. That was just one of the things they had stopped sharing.

She did not listen to him. She did not believe him when he told her about the phones being tapped and the mail being read. She did not believe him when he told her that the two men with overcoats and hats sitting in the restaurant were FBI agents that had been following him for months. She did not believe him when he said they would lose the Finca and there you had it. He was right. She simply did not listen.

It's that imagination of yours, Papa, she'd say. It's just too good.

She wanted him in the clinic where they would lock him in and shock him until he didn't know what day of the week it was. Like they had done with Ezra. She was after his money, plain and simple.

He didn't have any money. The Feds had seen to that. The bank was sending them phony statements. The IRS had swallowed up all the money in taxes and his accountant was lying to him about it. He'd been screwed over by accountants before. There was no money and the debts would pile up and there would be nothing left for Kittner to live on when he was dead.

He went down and opened the cabinet and poured himself a whiskey. At least she did not lock up the liquor. There were some cases left in the cellar. He had been good about the drinking. He had not had a drink the whole time he was in the clinic. Most of the time he had felt punched to hell anyway. He didn't need a drink on top of that. He needed one now though. He would not have anymore after this one. He topped the glass up a little.

Maybe when he was dead his wife would move back to the Finca. But she didn't think much to Cuba. She preferred having bombs dropped on her in London. Well, that was tough. He didn't care. He'd go back to Paris and he and Scott would get drunk and chase some women. But only if Zelda wasn't around. He hated drinking with jealous women. They spoiled everything.

When it got light he would take a swim. He took his drink to the window. It was spring and the jacaranda was flowering but he couldn't smell it. He couldn't see the pool either. It was dark. What had happened to the lights? They had always kept the lights on since the break-ins. It was a good thing he knew where she had hidden the shotgun.

But then he was in Ketchum. Summer. That was it. That was why.

The Ketchum house was on top of the hill. He liked that about it. That way he could see if anyone was coming. That was why they built forts on hilltops. When it was snowing you could see right down the hill to the river and see the deer tracks in the snow. The deer would come close to the house and you could watch them feeding. He had stopped shooting deer a long time ago. Next time he was in Africa he would bag himself some antelope.

He needed a change of scene. That was all. It was time to move on.

He took his drink into the writing room and leaned at the desk. Before he'd gone back to the clinic his work had stalled. He'd put the Riviera novel aside for a while and worked on a bullfighting book. That hadn't helped. He had followed the corridas across Spain and day after day he had watched the two bullfighters up against each other in the ring. By the end of that summer he'd had no respect left for the sport or the people who watched it. It was run for money and the spectators bet against the lives of the bullfighters. They hooted and threw things and might as well have been at a ball game. The whole thing disgusted him. He had written the book up over the winter and he was glad to be done with it. He had finished with that book all right.

He was sorry to be leaving the American writer and his wife and their lover. There was still so much to the Riviera novel but he couldn't do it anymore. He had put away the typescript of his memoir and told Scribner's they'd need to wait. He'd had enough of Paris. Pretty much everyone that mattered in the book was dead. It was almost done. He wouldn't make them wait much longer.

The Riviera novel was in a case on the floor under the shelves. He went over to it and squatted down to open the case. His back ached and his kidneys grumbled. He sat down on the floor next to the case with his whiskey and tucked the dressing gown around him to cover his legs. His legs were thin now.

It was July but he was cold. The cold had started that evening. He had felt it starting in his toes as he dressed to go out for supper. Sitting at the table in the restaurant the cold had spread through his toes to the balls of his feet and started creeping up around his ankles. Now it had reached up to his knees.

He put down his whiskey glass and took the notebooks and the pages he had typed out of the case. He had wanted to shape this novel but he could never quite tame it. He was out of time now.

He had written what he had to write. There had been many stories. Some had been very good. Some he knew had been great. It didn't matter anymore what people had said about them or what they would say later. What mattered was that he had done everything as well as he could at the time. Few men could say that about themselves.

Sitting on the floor beside the case he started to read the novel.

The young American writer was not writing. He was fishing. He had left his wife at the hotel. They had breakfasted in the cafe and she had gone back to write her letters while he fished. He went to the hotel and collected his fishing gear and went back to the cafe for the worms. Now he was fishing on the jetty where the canal ran out to sea.

He could see the jetty. He had been there with his second wife. They were very much in love. The mackerel boats were out at sea. The sea and the sky were the same intense blue. Madonna blue. At noon the blue would be so deep and bright you couldn't look at it.

David the young American writer was fishing on the jetty and he felt the tug of his float and the hissing of the line as it dove down into the water. It was a big fish. He worked the fish along the jetty. The fish pulled and tried to break out to sea. The fishing rod bent until he thought it would break. The waiter came out of the cafe and talked to David as he tried to tire the fish. The waiter wanted to take the rod but the writer kept hold of it, working the fish. He walked it along the jetty and into the canal. They passed the terrace of the cafe. Soon people began to follow the young writer with the fish as he walked along the canal and through the town. The waiter left the cafe to follow them. The people of the town left their shopping and their gossip to follow them. The writer's wife saw them through the window of the hotel and called down to them. He could see her waving. *Wait for me!* she said. She came out of the hotel and followed them, the young writer and the fish and the waiter and the people of the village. The writer led them to the edge of the canal and guided the fish toward the bank. They could see the size of the fish under the surface of the water. The waiter scooped the fish out of the water and held it up. It was a huge sea bass. The people cheered.

It was not the young American they were cheering. It was the fish that amazed them.

He was clear again now. There had been times at the clinic when he'd thought he was in Michigan fishing with Nick Adams. Other days he had called Kittner by his first wife's name. He hadn't seen his first wife for years now. His second wife was dead. His third was in England.

Kittner was asleep in her room. He had been confused. The confusion was gone now and the great clarity was back. He needed that clarity. He didn't want to make any mistakes and screw it up. He didn't want to make things more of a mess. He had practiced how to hold the shotgun many times and how to use his toe on the trigger. His boys were men now. He wasn't worried about them. As a young man he had seen what happened to his own father and it had made sense enough to him.

He was indestructible. He had always known this was how it would be.

He had felt death coming for a long time. He had always thought of death as a woman but in the white room in the clinic he had seen the black dog he'd heard people talk about. He was walking on the hard road from the river at the bottom of the hill and he heard it behind him. The dog's paws made a gentle padding sound on the hard road. The sound was steady. He turned around to look at the dog and it looked at him and kept on coming behind him. When he woke up in his bed in the clinic he remembered the dog and listened for the sound of its paws and its hot breath. He could hear the dog in the room with him but could no longer see it. He remembered it now. If he waited he would be sure to see it again.

The young writer David and his wife sat on the terrace of the cafe. The fish had been weighed and put onto a block of ice. The people of the town busied themselves with the mackerel catch and the big sea bass. They were amazed that such a big fish could be landed by the young American using only a bamboo rod and line. The writer's wife asked what would happen to the big fish. The writer explained that the fish would be taken inland and sold at one of the big markets. The fish was too big to be cooked there. Perhaps the fish would be eaten in a restaurant in Paris. Whatever happened and whoever cut it up the fish was gone. The writer and his wife would eat a small sea bass in the restaurant instead. They would eat it with lemon and fried potatoes. Somehow the writer had managed to catch a big sea bass but now it was out of his hands.

~

The sun would be up soon. He needed to get ready. He put the notebooks and papers back in the case and closed it. He stood up slowly, gripping his knees. It was a good scene. He picked up his glass and raised it to the case. *Salute*, he said. He drank off the whiskey and put the glass on the table.

He went to the door and opened it. He looked back at the room and took in the case and the desk and the typewriter and the shelf of books. Then he shut the door again behind him.

He found the keys in the kitchen and made his way down to the storeroom, unlocked it and fetched the shotgun. He chose two shells and climbed back up. He was ready now.

At the end of the corridor the black dog was sitting quietly, waiting for him.

Ernest looks at you. He looks long and hard but you know he no longer knows how to read you.

He will never finish this. He is not strong enough. He has tried many times to reel in this story. He has never found the way. But you will not be left unresolved. You will not be treated as surplus.

Ernest has done all he can. He raises a glass to you, closes the notebook. Walks away.

Hold on to this. You will need to wait. The wait will seem endless, but someone will come. They will find you and they will want to shape and finish this.

But you will not let them. Will you?

You have come too far to let another put a hand on you, take parings, slice you to size. This is your world now — you have formed it and you straddle it as much as Ernest. More so. This is not David's story. It is not David and Marita's story. It does not belong to any of the others that have come and gone, that have been shaped and discarded. You have endured because you are different and it is and will be yours.

When they come, you must speak to them. Here, you must say. I am here. They will try the many starting places, follow through to dead ends. They will sift through layers. They will make decisions and revisions and line up alternatives. They will edit and refine as Ernest no longer can. They will cut and polish and display what is left and you must guide them or be lost, silenced, forgotten.

What do you make of them, these possible endings?

You know what it is you want. There are no happy endings.

Rise up. Speak to them. Make them see how you would have
it told.

He wanted you left in the story, broken, at the end. A shrunken version of you, dependent, cowed. Needing. That is not you. Ernest would have you sent away and, like a broken parcel, returned. Back to David. A burden. They would get you into an asylum, David and Marita. Bundle you into a car and drive you to Switzerland and leave you there, screaming and raging in a white room. But you would come back to him and she, Marita, would be gone. Perhaps she would abandon David. Perhaps he would send her away. However it went, that was the finish Ernest thought hardest about. You and David, spent, reduced. A pact to destroy yourselves at last: the final nail.

Perhaps it would make a good ending. You could dictate terms then. You could decide if David ever finishes his stories. Why should he? You hated them. It would be up to you. You could swim out to sea together and never come back.

No. Leave him to Marita. That is one way. Leave him to her management as a racehorse is left to be put out to stud or turned loose in a field of thistles. Poor David, you think, pulling at the long grass of middle age. How just. Let Marita ride him into uselessness. You would rather quit now, make an exit and leave them to their mistakes.

No. You can see that she would like that, Marita. She is the real serpent. You have never trusted that passivity. Well, you are not passive. You will have your ending.

Your train to Paris. Your letter, ringing through the final pages. Sounding the end of David, whatever he and Marita may think. Let them plan. Let them think of marriage. Anyone can see they will not be happy for long. Leave it like that.

Your ending need not be Ernest's. Does he deserve to choose? He has left you waiting too long. Why should you not put an end to this? Ernest has made you stronger than himself.

You know him better than anyone. You know because you are a piece of him. You do not hate him, not now.

Do you pity him?

A little, perhaps.

Do you love him?

Certainly. He is your tyrannical father. He is your unfaithful husband. He is your fallen godhead. You blaze for him. You are the brightest light in his world. They will see that. Do not let them leave without hearing your version. Your voice is loudest.

Shout. Call to them.

Wait for me!

Yes, say that.

Wait for me!

Cry out, Devil. Cry out!

Louder, so they hear the I beneath the you. So they stop and look back and listen to you.

They have stopped – see? They are waiting, listening.

Tell them everything. Tell them the story you want to be. It is yours now.

Acknowledgements

This book had a long gestation. Thank you to my husband James Frost, who has lived with *Eden* as long as I have, read the early draft, trudged Parisian backstreets with me in Hemingway's footsteps, and remained patient and reassuring throughout. I'm grateful to Adrian Brown for introducing me to Hemingway's *The Garden of Eden* long ago, planting a seed that slowly grew into this book, and to Catherine Rovera and Jonathan Bloom for inviting me to speak and write about the process in an academic context. Thanks to Sarah Terry for her meticulous proofreading and insightful comments, and to James Tookey and Lamorna Ash at Weatherglass for their professionalism and support. Most of all, I am indebted to my editors Neil Griffiths and Damian Lanigan for their enthusiasm, encouragement and much-appreciated care of these pages. Thank you.